That One Left Shoe

an anthology

Edited by
Betsy A. Riley

Blue Dragon Press
All rights reserved.

ISBN-13: 978-0-9837356-6-3 (print version)
ISBN-10: 0983735662 (Blue Dragon Press)

ISBN-13: 978-1-62220-000-9 (eBook versions)

That One Left Shoe

an anthology

ACKNOWLEDGMENTS

Several people besides the authors have assisted in preparation of this anthology and the book marketing website, **ThatOneLeftShoe.com**. Most notably, Debra Eloise (**MyLadyEloise.com**) provided a number of photographs of left shoes, as did Alisa Piotrowski (**AlisaPiotrowski.com**). Alisa also created banner ads for the anthology and posted them on the web.

Betsy A. Riley served as organizer and editor of this project, publishing it under her imprint, **BlueDragonPress.com**. Betsy's brother Tom was the one who suggested opening the project to other authors, a great idea that lead to this robust collection. Proceeds from sales of the anthology by Blue Dragon Press are being donated to the Carroll County chapter of the Maryland Writers' Association. See the website for more info on the chapter (www.CarrollCountyMWA.org).

photo by Alisa Piotrowski

ONE LEFT SHOE
by Betsy A. Riley

That white tennis shoe on the side of the road,
what would we learn if its tale could be told?
Did it fly out a window, or fall off a truck,
did a one-legged hiker declare it bad luck?

Was it left as a sign to mark just this one spot,
or just left behind, with no sinister plot?
Is its mate down the road or offside out of view,
if we search just a bit might we re-pair the two?

It sits there so lonely, it's just one left shoe,
with no mate beside me, I'd be lonely too.

This poem was provided as inspiration to writers participating in this anthology project..

Betsy A. Riley is the organizer and editor of this anthology. She worked over 35 years at a National Laboratory before retiring to take a federal job in Maryland. Her publications represent invited lectures given across the U.S. and Europe, covering computer graphics, communication of new technology, and supercomputing. She has organized international scientific conferences and served as contributing editor for conference proceedings. In 2011, she published *The Comet*, an illustrated fable, and *Street People Tales*, a narrative poetry chapbook. In 2012, her poetry has been published in *Empirical Magazine*, *Pen in Hand*, and the anthology *Latitude on 2nd*. Betsy's short stories have been published in *Pen in Hand*, **Aspiring Writers 2011 Short Story Competition Winners Anthology**, and in other anthologies under other pen names. She is a member of the Eldersburg critique group, the Advanced Writing Workshop, the 270 Corridor Writers, the Maryland Writers Association and the Carroll County MWA chapter. Betsy's author website is brws.com

Betsy's entries include: "*One Left Shoe*," poem; "*The Patent Leather Predicament*," young adult humor; "*The Designer Sandals*," fiction humor; "*The Left Shoe*," lyrics; "*The Kudzu Conspiracy*," paranormal (writing as Delfina Hex); "*Slot Canyon Rules*" paranormal (writing as Delfina Hex); "*The Hand Painted Crocs*," drama (writing as Desdemona Pike); "*The Glass Slipper*," fantasy; "*The Glass Slipper Arrangement*," fantasy (writing as Delfina Hex)

collage by Betsy A. Riley

THE PATENT LEATHER PREDICAMENT
by Betsy A. Riley

I've always thought that I must have been swapped at birth, because I just don't fit in this family, anymore than I fit in the new patent leather shoes Mother bought me for Easter. Not that they aren't a nice bunch of people, but they're just different. Take my sister Jenna, or Fancy Nancy as I call her behind her back. She's the perfect little princess, the ultimate girly girl. She can sit perfectly still in church, and go through the whole day without mussing her dress or skinning a knee. Next to Jenna, I always feel rumpled and smudgy.

Jenna's just naturally neat and obedient. You might think that a girl like that would be a prig, but she's not. She's a really good big sister. She re-ties my hair ribbons for me when they come undone (which is about five minutes after Mother ties them). She loans me a clean handkerchief when I've spilt Kool-Aid on mine (which seems to happen anytime there is Kool-

Aid in the room). And she always carries Band-aids in her purse for when I skin a knee or elbow.

My folks are nice too. They don't seem to mind that I'm a Tomboy and am always getting my clothes grimy and torn. Father laughs and says I'm a stain magnet. Mother smiles and says I have unique charms all my own. I don't know what charms she means, unless it's that I'm really good at catching frogs.

My little brother Bobby is still a toddler and he has the longest curliest eyelashes you ever saw. I don't think it's fair. He's a boy and has those lovely lashes and I have stubby straight ones. His hair is blond and curly too, just like Jenna's, while I have plain brown hair that is straight as a stick. Just one more reason I'm sure I must have been switched at birth. Somewhere there's a family with klutzy, messy kids that's missing a middle sister, I just know it. And wherever they are, I bet those kids aren't wearing tight patent leather shoes.

Bobby still rides in a car seat, which only fits by the window, so I get stuck in the middle seat. Father smokes and flicks his ashes out the window and Mother is afraid they might blow in the back window and burn us. So Jenna sits on the left side, because they know they can trust her to keep the window closed. Sitting in the middle I get the breeze from both front windows and from Bobby's window. No wonder my hair is always a mess by the time we get to church.

I'm also supposed to watch Bobby during the drive. He likes to throw things out the window. Anything he can lay his hands on: his toys, Father's newspaper, the box of tissues. Once he even threw Mother's hat out the window after she made the mistake of laying it on the console while she adjusted a curl that had blown loose. But they never get mad at him, they just laugh.

It was Easter Sunday, one of my least favorite times of year. We all got new Sunday outfits for Easter, from head to toe. Which meant a new stupid hat with prongs that hurt my scalp, and a starched dress with lace trim that scratched my neck and arms. What I hated the most were the patent leather pumps. Mother had decided I was old enough to graduate from Mary Jane's to pumps. They were tight and hurt my toes. The shoe salesman swore you had to buy patent leather tight because it would stretch. Maybe it would if you wore it every day, but trust me, those Sunday shoes never stretched. They just got tighter and tighter until I couldn't even get them on. They made me feel like the ugly stepsister trying to squeeze into Cinderella's glass slipper.

The one thing I liked about Easter was the big egg hunt after church. This year I was finally old enough to search with the big kids, racing across the hayfield, where the eggs were almost invisible and the prize egg lay waiting. Up to now, I'd been stuck with the babies on the manicured lawn, where the eggs were just sitting out in plain sight. The shoes were going to ruin my big chance. It was bad enough being in the prissy dress, but no way could I run in those tight patent leather pumps. I'd begged and begged until finally Mother had agreed to let me bring my tennis shoes to change into after church

Mother stashed my tennis shoes in the trunk, but refused to let me add a pair of shorts and a tee shirt to change into. My feet were already hurting, and I swore I could feel blisters forming. Then I had a wicked idea. As I sat there between Jenna and Bobby, I wriggled my feet out of the tight shoes. I had to practically pry them off. I handed the first one to Bobby and crossed my fingers. He flung it out the window as expected, and neither Mother nor Jenna noticed. I waited to hand him the second one until we were crossing the low bridge over the creek. No one else noticed the silent splash. I stifled a laugh -- even if they decided to go back and look for the shoes, they'd never find the one in the creek.

I sat back in my seat and smiled, thinking how comfortable it would be to wear my tennis shoes to church. I knew Bobby wouldn't get in trouble, and I could just claim I didn't notice that he had my shoes until it was too late. All would be well. Then I looked up at the rear view mirror and saw Father's eyes watching me. I thought I was a goner, then he winked, and began singing "I gotta shoes, you gotta shoes, all of God's chillun got shoes . . . ." I'd never noticed before, but Father's hair is brown, and straight as a stick. Maybe I do belong in this family after all.

collage by Betsy A. Riley from photos by Debra Eloise

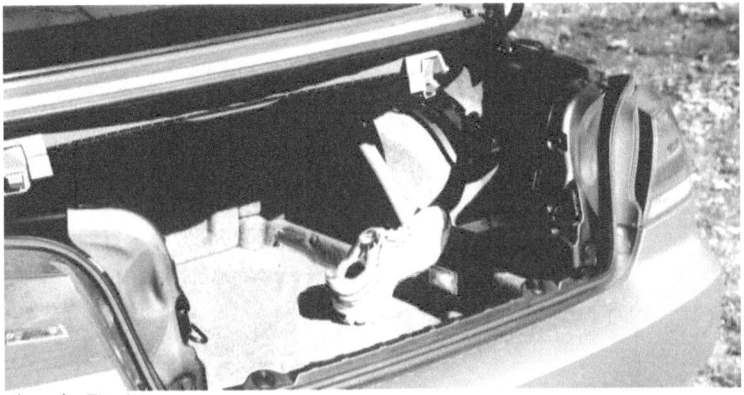

photo by Tim Jones

THE DESIGNER SANDALS

by Betsy A. Riley

Stop the car, stop the car!" I yelled, "pull over, pull over!"

Ralph screeched the brakes and swerved onto the shoulder, "What? What's wrong?"

"Didn't you see the red sole?" I said, "that was a Christian Louboutin shoe laying on the shoulder. Back up, I'll tell you when to stop."

"You've got to be kidding," Ralph said, "I'm not backing up on the interstate because you saw some weird shoe."

"Those weird shoes cost over a thousand dollars," I said, "and I'm just asking you to back up on the shoulder, so I don't have to walk back so far."

Ralph grumbled, but he backed the car up slowly. I was crossing my fingers that the mate to the shoe would be nearby. But if there was only the one, I'd still take it. I could put it on my desk to drool over while I worked. What can I say, I'm really into shoes, especially heels. Last time I counted, I had seventy-five pairs of shoes. That was counting everything, from beach thongs to snow boots. Not that bad, really.

Ralph was appalled at the number of shoes I had, but when I compared notes with my co-workers, I was in the minority. Jennifer had a hundred and sixty pairs, and Melinda had over two hundred. He doesn't complain too much, because he likes the way my legs look when I wear heels, and he knows I never pay full price. I'd never be able to score a pair of Louboutin's unless they just fell in my lap. This was my chance.

The shoe was gorgeous -- a black, lizard-skin strappy sandal, with the trademark red sole. I checked the bottom for the size and squealed with delight. It was my size! Oh, this was meant to be -- I just knew that the other shoe was out there waiting for me to find it.

It had been laying on its side on the edge of the shoulder, so the mate was probably off in the grass. Unfortunately the grass sloped away pretty steeply. No way I could do a good search wearing my peep toe sling back heels. They were really cute, red leather with a snappy bow, but I'd break an ankle if I tried to negotiate the slope in those heels.

I knew I still had an old pair of sneakers in the trunk, from the last time we went to the beach. I carried the Louboutin reverently to the car and asked Ralph to pop the trunk. "Isn't this just the most beautiful thing you've ever seen?" I said.

Ralph just rolled his eyes. "How long is this gonna take?"

"Till I find the other shoe," I said, "if you want it to go faster you could come help me search."

"I'll pass," Ralph said, rolling down the windows to catch a breeze and reclining his seat. "Wake me when you're done."

I rummaged in the trunk to find my sneakers, and sat on

the bumper to change shoes. I couldn't resist trying on the one shoe. It fit perfectly and looked fantastic on me. There was a scuff or two, probably from the asphalt shoulder, but I knew I could buff those out. Setting it carefully in the trunk next to my own heels, I donned my sneakers and prepared to search.

It was hot work. The asphalt radiated heat, and once I got down on the slope I lost the breeze. The grass had been trimmed so that I wasn't wading through weeds, but it was still tall enough to hide a shoe. I worked my way back and forth across the slope, painstakingly moving down about a foot on each pass. I knew the distance I had decided to cover was arbitrary, but I could just feel that shoe calling to me.

It was tougher when I reached the bottom of the slope. The ground leveled out, so the footing was easier, but the grass was taller and mixed with scrub bushes. Searching became more tedious, since there were so many hiding places. Sweat was trickling down my back, and my legs were starting to itch from brushing against the tall grass.

"Babe," Ralph called, "aren't you done yet? You might as well give up. The other shoe could be miles away. Come on."

I just couldn't give up. "Just a little longer," I shouted, and turned back to the line of brush. I squatted to view the terrain from a different angle, and that's when I saw the patch of red. I let out a whoop, and walked toward it in a crouch, afraid to stand lest I lose sight of my goal.

Eyes on the prize, I got close enough to verify that the patch of red was the sole of the matching shoe. Ralph was going to eat his words! Then I saw her. The woman lying just beyond the shoe. Her body was covered with bruises and scrapes from the tumble down the slope. I thought she must be dead and had a fleeting thought, wondering if the police would let me have the shoes, or if I could just slip them into the trunk before we reported the body. That would be wrong, but it was tempting. I shook my head to banish the thought. "No," I said to firm my resolve.

That's when the body moved. I screamed, then realized the woman was still alive as she began to moan. I shouted to Ralph, "Call 911, call 911--get an ambulance, there's someone here!" I went to the woman and crouched beside her, holding her hand. I was afraid to move her, and there was no gushing wound to put pressure on. So I just sat in the dirt and murmured, "It's okay, an ambulance is coming, you'll be fine." Mostly nonsense, but the sound of my voice seemed to soothe her, and she held on to my hand until the EMTs put her on a stretcher.

We had to stay behind, to tell the story to the police over and over. The beautiful shoes were taken as part of the evidence. The police wouldn't tell us anything. When it showed up on the news, we found out that the woman was a wealthy socialite who had been carjacked and abducted. In desperation, she had thrown herself from the moving car. The only mention of us was the report that a passing motorist had spotted her and called the police.

It was almost a month later when the big box arrived. I opened it to see rows of Louboutin shoe boxes, with a small envelope on top. The note read simply, *"Thank you for my life. Enjoy the shoes."*

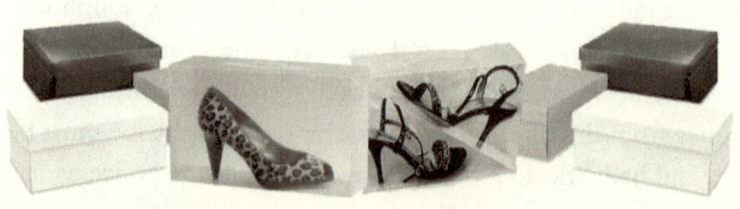

photo by Betsy A. Riley

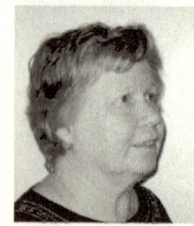 **Jo Donaldson** is currently experimenting with writing in different genres and recently completed a young adult novel, ***Crissy's Blizzard***. One of her short stories was chosen for the 2012 edition of ***Ginseng***, the literary publication of the Garrett County Arts Council. Jo was an award-winning staff writer for the *Cumberland Times-News*. As Public Affairs Officer for the Garrett County Chamber of Commerce and Press Officer for Garrett College, Jo wrote press releases for newspapers and magazines. She is a graduate of McDaniel College. She previously wrote for the *Carroll County Times*, *Hanover Evening Sun* and an aviation magazine, *Pilot's Preflight*. She is a member of the Maryland Writers Association and the Carroll County MWA chapter. Jo's website is www.kindredpens.com

Jo's entry, "*The Ruined Shoe*," is fiction. Her other pieces in this anthology are "*The Vet*," a poem with a non-fiction dedication, and "*One Shoe*," a non-fiction essay.

photo by Debra Eloise

THE RUINED SHOE
by Jo Donaldson

I can't believe it. How could he do this? It's destroyed." I hiccupped on the phone to my best friend Suzanne. "I can't stand it."

"Calm down. Everything will be fine. I'll be right over," she said.

She's also my neighbor. Two minutes later, she was there.

"You just sit down and take some deep breaths. I'll make some tea and you can tell me all about it."

She moved purposefully and soon we were sitting at my kitchen table, sipping hot, soothing Darjeeling in my Limoges tea cups. How could everything seem so normal? I wiped away a tear as I put the mangled shoe on the table. There it lay, on its side, a sorry sight.

"It's ruined, garbage," I cried.

"What happened? Tell me all about it," said Suzanne, taking my hand, while holding a cup of steaming tea in her other hand.

"It seemed so innocent when my son asked if I would watch his adorable little puppy while he went away for a weekend to enjoy the sun. It seemed so easy. I had a fenced yard for the puppy to run and take care of his business. In the beginning he slept peacefully, curled up on my favorite rug. But then...."

We looked at the back door, trying to ignore the barking and whining of the poor, pitiful pooch.

"Don't let him in. Don't be enchanted by those big, pleading brown eyes. That little Spitz is a demon in disguise. My slippers, tennis shoes, pillows, have all felt the force of those canine teeth. What inner fury causes him to destroy?"

"You are getting too dramatic," she said. "Sip your tea."

"I can't help it. He is a destroyer of all that is beautiful, a mini demon," I said. Then I paused, inhaled the relaxing aroma and felt the warmth on my face. "Why didn't he ruin one of my older shoes? Why choose my favorite pair for his pacifier? I was planning to wear these to the benefit next week."

I tossed the mangled shoe at the back door. The loud thump momentarily halted the puppy's whining. I put the other shoe on the table and took another sip of tea.

"It's so beautiful, but it's all alone now. This is all that is left of that perfect pair, so comfortable, so chic, so perfect for an evening on the town. What can I do with one left shoe?" I moaned. "I only have the one shoe left. "

"Use it for a flower pot? Who cares? This is easy to fix," Suzanne said, grabbing the tea cups and putting them in the sink. "Let's go shopping. They are having a sale at The Shoe Emporium and they have both left and right shoes."

A few minutes later and we were out the door. Good friends, they know what you need.

illustration by Allie Hylton, www.alluregraphicdesign.com

 **Kerry Peresta** was born in Augsburg, Germany, and has lived all over the United States and overseas, compliments of a father who chose the Air Force as his career. She has recently moved to Reisterstown, Maryland with her husband after a two-year contractual obligation in Pierre, South Dakota. She attended high school in Little Rock, Arkansas and achieved a Bachelor of Science in Commercial Art from Arkansas State University. After a 25-year advertising career and raising four children and numerous cats, Kerry transitioned to full-time writing as a career focus. She is currently employed as a Technical Writer in the Baltimore area; and is a published humor columnist. Her work has been published in newspapers, magazines, and e-zines. Most recently, her articles have been picked up by Empty Nesting Magazine Online. She has completed her first novel, and is involved in the query process. Kerry's website is www.emptynesting.webs.com.

Kerry has two entries, "*The Toad Lady*," humor, and "*Princess*," a romance.

photo by Debra Eloise

THE TOAD LADY

by Kerry Peresta

The storm finally blew over and the sun shone brilliantly through the clouds; like splashes of gold in a muck of pea soup. It had been raining on and off for two weeks, and the entire town of Toad Suck seem to smell slightly of mold.

The mood in Cleo's Cafe was grumpy, but like the weather, seemed to be clearing. Billy Barnes, a regular at Cleo's every day around 4:00, scraped back his stool from the counter, wiped his mouth with the back of his hand and declared that afternoon's fresh-baked scones a real triumph. Yep, almost as good as a few years ago, he thought, and glanced at a framed photo of a gorgeous young woman holding a tray of Danishes conspicuously placed on the wall behind the counter. He patted his paunch appreciatively, picked up a toothpick, and winked at the picture.

Cleo's Grocery and Cafe was a well-known, historical landmark in Toad Suck, Arkansas, a community of 2367 hardy souls who didn't mind drenching humidity every summer and blood-sucking hordes of mosquitoes. Because the town was located on the Arkansas River, the inevitable tendency to groundwater accumulation created the perfect breeding ground for mosquitoes. Toad Suckers had no choice but to endure the occasional buzzing black cloud all summer. They put up with it because the river was a big attraction for river floaters and fishermen and such and without it Toad Suck would probably not exist; nor would it boast the Toad Suck Festival, a huge annual spring event that brought in hundreds of thousands in revenue to the tiny town.

The bell over the Cafe' entrance clanged. Billy shifted the toothpick to the other side of his mouth, observed the man with friendly interest, and invited him to sit beside him with his eyes.

"Hey there," Billy said, extending a calloused hand, "how are ya today? New around here?" The man smiled and shook hands with Billy.

"Rob Posey."

"Name's Billy. Billy Barnes. Passing through or stayin'?"

"Passin' through," Rob said as he pulled out a stool and took a seat. He turned over his coffee cup and nodded at the young woman behind the counter to fill it. " I heard about this town, Toad Suck, and some kind of story about a woman and a festival…the Toad Suck Festival, right? Where people bring in toads and race them?" He smiled and sipped his coffee. "Thought it would be interesting to see the town."

Billy smiled broadly. Adrenaline coursed through his aging veins as he anticipated a willing listener. "Well," he said, and indicated the picture on the wall with a nod, "the story is all about that woman up there on the wall."

"You knew her?" Rob asked, eyebrows raised.

"Oh yeah," Billy said. "I was one of her best customers!"

"Mind telling me the story?"

And so Billy Barnes got up from his stool and indicated the man should follow him over to a table in the corner, where he began; as many times before, to tell this story.

"When she took a job at this here Café, and settled in to live in the little apartment behind this place, people scratched their heads. Couldn't quite figure out what drew her to Toad Suck, what with all that youth and beauty and talent. But stay she did, and she worked right here in this room. 'Course it's been redone some, because there was a fire, but I'm gettin' ahead of myself. Her name was Lynette Blackwell, and she could make scones and pastries and such better than anything I have ever tasted, and that's a fact." Rob quietly pulled out a pad and pen. Billy didn't seem to notice that the man was taking notes, and he relaxed into the pleasant memories. He could still hear her voice…

"Bye now, y'hear? Ya'll don't forget that tomorrow I'll be baking up some fresh cherry Danishes, and maybe some fried peach pies. Be sure and bring your friends, now," Lynette said. She gave Billy her cheeriest smile, waved, jiggled her bosom at him a bit, and turned back to washing dishes behind the counter of the charming country café in a detached converted garage behind Cleo's Grocery.

She was such a pretty little thing; shiny, brown hair and strong young legs that she liked to show off, which accounted for a pretty brisk business at Cleo's Café. The owners of Cleo's, Ron and Louise, hired her even though they were a little suspicious because they never could get her to tell them much about her past. After a while, didn't matter at all though, because that girl could bake like nobody's business. The whole town smelled like a French pastry shop every afternoon.

Before long, Lynette asked Ron and Louise if she could wear a toad costume in the Café while she was baking in honor of the upcoming Toad Suck Festival. They agreed, but Louise grumbled about how revealing her costume was. Since Ron was pretty excited about all the new customers she was bringing in, he was not concerned about her skimpy costume. Money was money.

When the annual Toad Suck Festival came around in the spring, Lynette baked extra in anticipation of the event. She'd decided to take her melt-in-your-mouth Danishes and her toad costume and plunk herself down in the Cleo's Grocery and Café booth she'd convinced Ron to sponsor. Her booth was real popular, especially when she exited and bent over to refresh her collection of goodies. Toad Suckers cluck-clucked over the revealing toad costume, but they didn't cluck too much because she was making Cleo's a fair amount of money; plus she was drawing out-of-town business as well. All in all, Toad Suckers felt pretty honored that Lynette had chosen their town to bless with her considerable assets.

Soon people were showing up from Little Rock and Bentonville and El Dorado with cameras in search of the "Toad Lady." *Arkansas Magazine* contacted Cleo's for an interview. Lynette became an official local celebrity and Ron and Louise doted on her like proud parents.

Lynette began wearing a different toad costume every day. Ron and Louise agreed to allow her to flounce about in the skimpy – albeit rather adorable – toad costumes because their profits were now through the roof. They even had a "Toad Lady Inside, Hop On In!" sign made with a big red arrow pointing to the back of Cleo's Grocery that led to the entrance of the Café where Lynette busily pushed dough into quaint shapes and hefted trays into the oven. When she fully committed to the toad theme by fashioning frog-shaped pastries, she felt somewhat blissfully centered, as though she had stumbled on to her very purpose in life. Lynette was well on her way to pastry heaven, theoretically speaking.

During an especially busy day, her phone jangled in her pocket. She let the call go to voicemail. For one thing her hands were dusty with flour and she had been sneezing through flour clouds all morning. The call could wait.

Finally, she heaved the last tray of toad Danishes in the oven, reminded herself to make sure she set the timer, swept her hair out of her face (which was charmingly encrusted with bits of dough), and returned the call. Through the pastry bits and the inevitable face-dusting of flour, one could not really tell, but she turned sheet-white as she listened. She stumbled to a chair in the corner behind the counter, and buried her face in her hands.

She'd hoped the nightmare on the other end of the call was behind her. Her mind raced toward hypothetical consequences, each one bashing into the other in a cacophony of nerves. Her stomach began to heave and she felt slightly dizzy, and then...blackness as she slipped to the floor in a dead faint.

A couple hours later Ron sniffed something burning, and saw smoke curling in under the door. Ron caught Louise's eye over the produce section – the cabbages and the turnips – and they instantly mind-melded the same thought: impending doom. They had been married long enough to share one mind, so no words needed to be spoken at this moment. As one, they raced to the Cafe. Louise glanced knowingly at Ron as if to say,

"I told you this couldn't last. Besides, her costume is ridiculous." He sighed as he ran, having heard this at least 437 times before.

They slid to a stop before the Café and jerked open the door. There was no one at the counter. Smoke and tiny licks of flame spiraled out of the huge twin ovens. Ron glanced meaningfully at Louise and she correctly interpreted the glance as, "Call 911! Now!" and ran to the phone. Ron batted through the smoke to turn off the ovens, and tripped over something blocking his way behind the counter. He squinted through the smoke, peered at the obstruction and screamed, "Oh my God! Lynette!" He reached down and picked up her inert form, toad costume and all; staggered out the door into the grocery office, and deposited her on the couch. He knelt beside her, patted her face, and tried to ignore the awkwardly-splayed long, muscled legs begging for his appreciative gaze. Legs, he soon discovered, that were attached to an attractive, toad-costumed corpse. He hung his head as tears seeped from the corners of his eye. After a few minutes, he rose, slapped the tears from his face, located an extra tablecloth to cover her, and walked from the room.

Billy paused for a sip of coffee and locked eyes with the stranger taking meticulous notes. Rob paused, pen in mid-air, and regarded him for a long moment. Billy pointedly stared at the notes on the pad. Rob reached into his pocket and slipped out a hundred dollar bill. Smooth as a whistle, Billy palmed the bill, tucked it into his shirt pocket, and resumed his story.

The whole town turned out for Lynette's funeral. The Toad Suck Festival Committee showed up all decked out in toad hats, and people left all manner of toad figurines and such at the door of the Café. Odd though, that Ron and Louise could not find one single family member to mourn her passing. She was buried not too far from Cleo's Grocery and Café, and her gravestone read "Here lies the Toad Lady of Toad Suck. She is now baking with the angels." The stone was dyed to a greenish hue in honor of her high calling. Looked a little like mold, but still, it's the thought that counts. That evening, the toad song seemed louder than usual. Everyone commented on it.

After the smoke cleared (so to speak), folks were shocked to find out that their Toad Lady had worked as a lady of the evening for a good ole' boy out of Memphis that ran a group of gals over in Mountain Home. No one would have been the wiser, except for an unsolved murder case over there that got re-opened because police found one of her shoes. A green, high-heeled shoe, stuck deep in mud, right where the good ole' boy from Memphis had been fished out from the lake real bloated and real dead. Truth be told, nobody much cared that this fellow turned up dead; he was mean and used those gals, but justice would take its course.

Ron and Louise and the Toad Suck Festival Committee decided unanimously that something had to be done to protect the town's reputation. So a plan was hatched.

They went to her little apartment, looking for potential evidence that would implicate her in the murder. The place was neat as a pin, but smelled real moldy, they noticed. After a bit of searching, darned if they didn't find the mate to the shoe the police found! After a hushed, secret meeting they decided to take most of Lynette's worldly goods and bury them in the woods. A couple of burly Toad Suckers skulked through the night with two big trash bags full of clothes and shoes and make-up and such and buried them good and deep. Detectives that came around askin' questions later couldn't find enough evidence to convict the dead girl, so they left. The town heaved a sigh of relief.

Now here's the part that everybody clammed up about when those detectives came snoopin': as the body was being prepared for burial, examination revealed a condition known as "syndactyly," or webbed feet; and behind Lynette's ears were small openings that appeared to be gills.

Billy paused and shrugged as he anticipated Rob's reaction. Rob put his pen down, crossed his arms and stared at Billy. Neither spoke for a long moment.

"You think she was part *toad* . . . is that what you're saying?" Rob said.

Billy looked Rob in the eye. "She loved those toad costumes. She was right pretty in 'em. And toad Danishes? Why would she bake those?" He pointed at the rows of toad Danishes, now quite famous, poised alertly on shelves behind the counter; a duplication of Lynette's efforts. "Everyone knew she loved to swim; she could swim like a fish! And her place…well, folks said it always smelled real moldy in there, like pond scum." He shrugged again, and looked out the window.

Rob stifled a grin. Billy had saved his ace in the hole for last, though, and proceeded to wipe the grin off the stranger's face. "Remember that shoe they found?" Rob nodded.

"Well, one just like it was found floating in the river during last year's festival. The left one. Same size, same color. When it was fished out, the toads on the banks of the river kicked up a fuss like you wouldn't believe. Inside the shoe was a little toad figurine stuck way down at the end."

"Great story," said Rob, thinking he had at least a week of verification and research ahead of him; but already outlining the article he'd planned for *Southern Living Magazine*. "Thanks for your time," he said and abruptly rose. Billy dipped his head in acknowledgment and tilted in his chair on its back legs as he watched the stranger leave.

After the door banged shut, Billy smiled and muttered to himself, "Can't believe every single one of them dang writers that come through here believe all that crap." He pushed himself up off the chair, grinned at Lynette's picture, fingered his shirt pocket, and went home a happy man.

photo by Debra Eloise

 **Sara Van der Wansem** was born in Mexico City, Mexico. Her primary language is Spanish. Sara is retired and enjoys making dolls and has a large collection of dolls and clowns. In Mexico, Sara graduated from the *Instituto Mexicano Norteamericano de Relaciones Culturales*. She also graduated from the At Home Professions Medical Language and Transcription program, of Fort Collins, Colorado Sara enjoys writing her memoirs, short stories, and poetry. She contributed monthly articles to a local bilingual newspaper in Moultrie, GA, where she was a successful administrator of a Migrant Head Start Center. Sara is member of several writing and poetry groups.

Sara's entry, *"Maggie and the Train,"* is a fictionalized memoir, as told to Betsy A. Riley.

MAGGIE AND THE TRAIN

by Sara Van der Wansem
as told to Betsy A. Riley

Maggie loved riding the train, especially now that she was almost eighteen and permitted to travel alone, it made her feel all grown up, exotic and adventurous. She liked to pretend she was Greta Garbo, playing the spy Mata Hari. She'd imagine herself on a mysterious mission, carrying a secret message. For this trip, though, she was traveling to visit a friend who was ill, so she became Little Women's Josephine March, as played by Katherine Hepburn. She pretended she was rushing home from New York City to the sickbed of her little sister Beth.

In the small town that was Maggie's destination, another young girl was playing make believe. Rebecca was leading a group of local children who had gotten bored during their summer vacation. Rebecca had decided to pretend they were fugitives, escaping from a foreign prison. At first they jogged single file down the side of the road, ducking behind trees when they saw a farm wagon or truck. After a while, that got boring, so Rebecca declared that they should cross the road in front of the vehicles, as if they were fleeing timber wolves.

Nobody wanted to be eaten by imaginary timber wolves, so they followed Rebecca's lead, and found it was surprisingly easy to dash across in front of even the automobiles. The children didn't notice that most of the vehicles were already slowing down because of the railroad crossing just ahead. When Rebecca heard the whistle of the train, she proposed that they run across in front of the engine. "It's a classic escape move," she said, "we cross in front of the train at the very last minute, and then the people chasing us have to wait for the whole train to go by before they can follow." The other children refused to do something so risky, they'd rather pretend the train was a fire-breathing dragon and run away from it screaming. But Rebecca was determined to have her way, even if she had to go it alone.

Maggie was tired and the constant rocking of the train had almost lulled her into a doze, when the train's whistle began to blow nonstop. The engineer had applied the emergency brakes, and there was a loud screeching and the passengers were thrown from their seats at the sudden drop in speed.

When the train came to a complete stop, the passengers crowded out to see what had happened. There were murmurs of "the train hit a kid" being passed back from the front of the crowd. Maggie joined the group, making her way to the front of the train. There the passengers spread in a wide circle, many turning their faces away from the center of attention. Twelve-year-old Rebecca lay sobbing on the ground. She kept calling out to the crowd, "My shoe, please give me my shoe."

Maggie could not stand the pitiful crying, so she called out, "Please, someone give it to her."

One man turned around and said, "Why don't YOU give it to her."

Maggie looked around and spotted a black leather shoe that laced up to the ankle sitting in the middle of the tracks. She started towards it, only to realize that the girl's foot was still encased in the shoe, which lay in a pool of spurted blood. To her shocked eyes, the foot seemed to jerk with a life of its own.

The image would haunt Maggie's dreams for years, and it took away her enjoyment of train rides.

photo by Debra Eloise

**Reggie Greenberg** has been writing stories, songs and poems since age five. She has been published in *Washington Post Magazine*, *Calvary Baptist News* and *Maryland Pet Profiles*. She is currently working on a memoir. Reggie is a member of the Eldersburg Critique Group.

Reggie's entry, "*The Missing Shoe,*" is a fictional account of a cold case still open in Baltimore County, Maryland. The names have been changed.

photo by Debra Eloise

THE MISSING SHOE
by Reggie Greenberg

A Wicked Witch of the West shoe, black with a chunky heel, poked out of a pile of plowed, soot-speckled snow at the intersection. No sign of a green-faced Margaret Hamilton swooping down to snatch the ugly thing, and no spell-casting smoke filled the air. Only the exhaust from our tailpipe hovered behind us as my mom shifted our green '68 Camero into gear and accelerated away from the stop light. The lone leather shoe diminished to a black dot in the side mirror as we sped toward Archbishop Keogh High School. I arrived for school late as usual. It wasn't the best way to begin the New Year.

Those shoes made me think of Sister Celia, my music teacher during my first semester at Keogh. Her shoelaces were unmatched, one blue and one black. No one noticed, except me. After I told her, she rectified the problem the next day. I felt like we had this secret bond after that.

During the spring of that same year, I witnessed her having an argument. I had gone to get my gym shoes out of my locker, which was right next to the chaplain's office. I saw Sister Celia through the partially open door. Her hands frantically darted in front of Father Joe's face like humming birds. Her voice sounded like a squeaky door hinge, but I couldn't really hear what she was saying. Father Joe's fist unclenched as he reached past her. She turned and I could see her eyes and nose were all blotchy and red. His unyielding smile looked as straight as a pink pencil, as he pushed the door shut.

Sister Celia transferred to another school shortly after that. Gossip about Father Joe flowed like a cesspool.

"He keeps a pistol on his desk," my friend Theresa had said.

"He only counsels the druggies and the sluts," someone else had said.

The following fall, I spied Sister Celia at the shopping center near school. It was October 7th or 8th because I had gone shopping with my dad to get Mom an anniversary present. Dad always waited until the last minute to do everything.

Sister Celia hurried out of the department store. She stopped briefly, slid her handbag over her arm, and pushed a small grey bag into the pocket of her navy blue wool coat. Her car keys glinted in the autumn sun as she brushed windblown strands of brown hair from her face. I couldn't believe she still wore those unflattering shoes with regular clothes. They looked oddly out of place with her outfit, a plaid skirt and white blouse.

She met a dark haired man at her car. I recognized him from freshman retreat at Manresa in Annapolis. He had provided security that weekend. He helped Sister Celia unlock the passenger side door of her Dodge. As soon as she hustled into the seat, he reached over and fastened her seatbelt, like she was some invalid. Then he limp hopped over to the driver's side, jumped into the seat and drove up the hill. I could see the red brick facade of the Distillery in the distance. They made whiskey and other things there that Catholics weren't supposed to drink.

I didn't think much about Sister Celia anymore until February. That's when the newspaper said that a hunter stumbled onto a woman's frozen partially decomposed body in the woods up by the Distillery. A prescription bottle inside her purse identified the ice cold corpse as that of Sister Celia. One of her uniform shoes lay beside her in the snow.

photo by Debra Eloise

The Vet
By Jo Donaldson

He said it didn't matter
What he left behind,
A soldier doesn't flee from danger
and it does no good to whine.

But it's hard to understand
What he must go through
When all he needs to buy
Is one left shoe.

Jo: *This poem was inspired by my father and other veterans like him. He had to wear a special built-up shoe because of wounds sustained in World War II. His wounds never healed, yet he helped raise four kids, worked, farmed and was a boy scout leader. Later in his life he worked with veterans' organizations, helping other veterans to receive the benefits they deserved. He always said he was one of the lucky ones. He was able to come home.*

photo by Debra Eloise

ONE SHOE
by Jo Donaldson

The horrible image of one shoe in a smashed up convertible still haunts me. One shoe was all that I saw in the remains of a car that carried seven teenagers to their deaths. One shoe brings back a decades old memory. The pieces flit through my mind. I remember the newspaper articles, the adults talking about the tragedy, the shoe and a lost friend.

A fast car, alcohol, teenagers and a race. Two cars speeding down a tree lined country road. Then the road turned, but one car didn't. The car plowed down several trees before stopping. Five young lives ended immediately, two lingered a little longer. How fast were they traveling to have been thrown out of the car and even out of their shoes?

They towed the death car to a junk yard near my home. I saw it there. My brother said there were several shoes left in the convertible. But that brown loafer was all I saw before I turned away. That image still haunts me. Was that my friend's shoe? She used to wear loafers with white socks. She wanted to have fun and excitement. She wanted to be a grown-up. It only took a moment as the speeding car left the road and met a tree, and she would never grow up.

It was all over the news in our rural county. Adults used the accident as an example for us: not to drink and drive, and not to speed, if we didn't want to die young.

Thinking about one shoe moved my friend forward in my memory files. I knew her best from the Westminster Airport where her father was an instructor. I went to a party or two at her house, but when my parents found out there was some smoking and drinking involved, I couldn't go to her parties anymore.

She is not pictured in my high school yearbook. So, I look up her photo in my Junior High School year book. Yes, that is how I remember her; a cute, brown-haired, happy girl who died too young.

photo by Debra Eloise

photo by Betsy A. Riley

 **Andy Gerb's** passion for writing fiction dates back to the first grade. He wrote his first story in crayon at age six, and hasn't stopped since. He holds a bachelor's degree from Brown University and a graduate degree from Stony Brook University. He currently lives in Maryland with his wife and their two children. He is a member of the Eldersburg critique group.

Andy's entry, *"Does He Know?,"* is a psychological drama.

photo by Debra Eloise

DOES HE KNOW?

by Andy Gerb

D oes he know?
We were called to a three car pileup on the
ramp to the interstate. One of the vehicles, a green
pickup, had spun into a concrete support. When we got there,
flames were dancing around the bed, and we doused them
quickly before they spread to the other vehicles.

That was fine. It was all fine. Everything was fine until we
were packing to go back. Tows had already dragged the wrecks
from the scene. An ambulance had evacuated the two injured
passengers (None serious. Thankfully, seatbelts were used all
around), and only we and the patrol car remained.

That's when Sam, our squad leader, noticed the shoe.

A ladies' pump, smooth black leather, lay at the edge of
the grass leading up the steep bank. Maybe one of the
victims left it behind, or maybe it sat for weeks waiting to be
found.

The highway patrolman, climbing into his cruiser, denied knowing anything about it. That's when Sam turned to us.

"Maybe it's Ben's," he said smiling at me.

Nobody could accuse him of unfriendliness. Harmless ribbing, that's all he'd have to cop to, were he on some witness stand. But I detected a fleeting coldness in his eyes. Or thought I detected. Or imagined. Or maybe it wasn't there at all.

But I remembered seeing those lace curtains move.

Does he know?

There are eighty muscles in the human face. Or thirty. Or twenty. I don't remember exactly, but the point is there are a lot. And at that moment I was straining to keep every one completely still. Not a twitch. Not a spasm. No sign that I took his remark as anything but lighthearted foolishness. Do you know how hard that is? Try it. Put on a facial expression. A smile, a frown, anything. Then freeze there, not moving, not letting a single jiggle or flicker squeeze through.

The hot, embarrassed flush engulfing my cheeks and forehead certainly didn't help.

Even as I was hiding my inner turmoil, I was examining Sam's face. Or trying to without letting him know I was looking. What did he know? Was he just playing with me, or had he heard something? Or figured something out? Or both? His eyes told no tales as he turned away and carelessly tossed the shoe back onto the dirt. I turned away also, trying to look casual. Trying not to keep wondering what Sam knew or guessed. And trying to stop thinking about the lace curtains.

Does he know?

Is this the beginning of something? Is my tenure at the Grain Valley Volunteer Fire Corps to deteriorate into a downward spiral of innuendos and implications, taunts and digs? Will I need to quit the Corps and crawl into my bed to hide from the shame?

When I was five, playing in our front yard, a fire siren screamed along our road. I turned toward the engine before it disappeared behind a bank of trees, and glimpsed the crew frantically adjusting equipment and scrambling to be ready for whatever fire they were rushing to fight. How exciting, I thought then and many times since, to be ready at a moment's notice to leap on a truck and prepare for urgent rescue. I joined up the day I turned eighteen, though not yet through my senior year. It didn't matter. I'd have joined earlier if allowed.

Was this all to end because of those infernal lace curtains?

photo by Debra Eloise

Does he know?

My mother doesn't, whose basement I inhabit while saving meager earnings from the Men's Clothing department at Walmart (my day job, I call it). My father doesn't suspect, when I visit him and his live-in girlfriend just over the state line. I was even smart enough not to tell Reverend Hartmann. No, until recently the sole keeper of my secret was Ira, the leader of the church youth group. Six years ago at age 13, I opened up to him about feelings toward several other boys in the group.

"Those feelings come from the devil, Ben," Ira told me. "You must never act on them. That would be a sin against God. Whenever you find yourself thinking that way, you must pray that the Lord protects you from these feelings. Do you understand?"

I did understand. And I didn't need Ira's warnings to know the social consequences of an embarrassing revelation. I progressed through school, played sports and did anything else that kept me busy. After graduation, I worked extra shifts whenever Walmart needed me, and filled my remaining time volunteering at the firehouse. My thoughts were private, and if I stayed busy, nobody would know. Nobody would talk. It was fine. For all I know, it might still be fine. I wish I was sure about those lace curtains.

Does he know?

Todd knew. I don't know how. He shrugged when I asked him, not taking the question seriously. He could do no better than, "I sorta felt it."

Todd works in housewares. He wasn't from our school, so I saw him first when he stopped by my display to sample the latest men's T's. It was the first of many visits that morphed into habitual lunch breaks together.

I hoped. Oh boy, did I hope. But I didn't know.

I did know that Todd is precious. That's my word for him. Precious. You'd consider yourself fortunate to know him. Life continually fascinates him. He'll tell you anything about himself, and it'll sound like literature. He'll listen to your stories and notice things even you didn't. I came to anticipate our daily lunches with more eagerness, even, than my firehouse shifts. That was before the lace curtains   .

Does he know?

Or was Sam just needling me about the woman's shoe being mine, to see me react. Our squad leader is like that. He was two grades ahead of me, the starting quarterback when I was a third string receiver, that one year I tried football, before realizing that being slammed to the ground dozens of times was not for me. He was always throwing barbs, even at his friends. "Making sure they're tough enough," I once heard him say, when someone called him on it. "Surround yourself with only the toughest, only the strongest, only the best."

If he knows about me now, does he still think I'm the toughest, the strongest, the best?

Todd came by menswear three days ago waving the newest version of Hell Drivers. The original shrink wrap still surrounded it, as if protecting us from the kinetic flaming cars on the cover of the video game. He casually offered an invitation to his apartment to be the first to play it. I didn't dare expect anything other than a friendly visit. Not driving over, not climbing the stairs to his landing, nor knocking on his door. Hope first glimmered on the couch facing his game console. I settled at the far right end just against the sofa's arm. I expected him at left end, but instead he lowered himself right next to me. We weren't touching, but so close you could not comfortably have inserted a finger into the separation between his jeans and mine.

He looked up at me. Amazing eyes. How can I describe them? Open to the world, vast, expansive, flooding the universe with light. His face just hinted at a smile, as if anticipating the punch line of a fascinating story without knowing exactly how it will end.

He didn't kiss me. I kissed him first. It was a risk. I knew it was a risk. Even with his deliberate proximity, I still doubted. I was putting a valuable friendship on the line, my most valuable ever. But I couldn't *not* kiss him. If you've been there, you know. He was close. He was beautiful. Things could go no other way.

I don't know when we finally slept. It was certainly after his clock glowed 3:30AM in the darkness of his room where we retreated after the kiss, Hell Drivers still in the console never launched. I had not intended to stay late; I had a morning shift the next day. But I'd never had such a night. I might never have another. I wanted to make it last.

When we woke, the sun was up. I dressed quickly for work. At the door, Todd gave me a prolonged kiss followed by a stroke on my shoulder. "Don't worry," he told me. "We'll pick up where we left off."

I dashed outside, hoping no one would see me. As I stepped onto the concrete landing, there was already too much sunlight to allow an escape into darkness. I looked around at the still windows of the neighboring apartments. What people lived there? I didn't know. I probably knew several – friends, friends of friends, people at my church, my school, or shoppers where I worked. Todd's screen door slipped out of my hand and slammed behind me, brick walls echoing its loud clang.

It was then I saw the lace curtains. At my vision's edge, I glimpsed a flicker of movement in one of the windows. I whirled in time to watch the curtains swing closed, as if someone quickly withdrew their face from their central seam.

"Disregard it," I told myself. "It's probably someone's cat. Or a draft." But the notion haunted me that behind those lace curtains, someone noticed I'd stayed the night at Todd's.

Does he know?

Does everyone? Did someone tell a bunch of friends, who

told a bunch of friends, and now the world knew what I did? Everything I did. Every shameful, shocking, beautiful, delicious move Todd and I shared? Did my mother know? It would kill her. Would the couple in the next pew at Sunday services whisper? Did everyone at Walmart know? My boss? My coworkers? Roxanne Templeton who rang up my occasional bag of chips in the express checkout? Roxanne, who in school was the source of every single rumor. Roxanne, of whom it was jokingly said, "today Roxanne, tomorrow the world" referring to her inclination toward juicy gossip.

Could I face that? Could I face everyone knowing what kind of person I am, the things I'm driven to? What to do? Move away? Commit suicide? Walk around with my face in a constant state of guilt and shame? If it works out, I'll have Todd. That's something. More than something. Maybe something great. But is it enough?

Does he know?

photo by Debra Eloise

photo by Debra Eloise

photo by Betsy A. Riley

PRINCESS

by Kerry Peresta

Lila stopped at the water's edge to pick up a shell and stuff it in the pocket of her windbreaker, shivering a bit in the dawn breeze. The sun was just starting to peek above the ocean, which was gray instead of blue-green today. She shaded her eyes and peered upwards, noting the dark clouds were stubbornly refusing to budge. Just like her mood.

Once a year she made the trek to this beach; a white-sanded, cocoon of a place. It had become a ritual. This was the fourth year. She bent and reached for another shell and rubbed its surface with her fingers, noting the pearlescent interior when she turned it over. This one, too, was slipped into her pocket. Out of the corner of her eye, she saw a sand crab scuttle sideways. He didn't expect people out this early, she thought. She smiled, and walked on.

Five years ago, her family had buried her twin sister, and she'd felt like a limb had been amputated. To this day, she lived

47

with phantom pain. Walking the beach where they had shared so many happy times helped. Her hands nestled against the seashells in her pockets. The sun was half-way up now; she could feel its warmth begin to seep through the chill. She quickly pulled the band from her wrist and secured her hair, which was whipping around her face in the breeze. She smiled at the memory of her sister doing the same thing on this very beach.

After shaking her fist at God the first few months, she had settled into a barter tone with Him. She asked Him to tell her sister how much she was missed, and let her know she'd never forget her. Not ever. Then she tentatively asked if she could somehow communicate with her, and promised that she would attend church regularly if He would consider this. Her cheeks had turned bright red, and she'd been surprised at her reaction, and figured it was because the request had been inappropriate so she never brought it up to Him again.

Her sister, Kyla, had been everything she was not. It was as if you took the same girl and cloned her, but with a completely opposite personality. Where Kyla was extroverted, daring, charming and popular, Lila was shy and bookwormish. The differences became most obvious in their shared college experience, where Kyla pledged a sorority and became a sought-after date for fraternity functions; and Lila shunned the Greek community and spent weekends in the library or drove home. She was not jealous of her sister, but did sort of depend on her to prop her up in social situations. They talked of trading places sometimes, to play a joke on some of Kyla's boyfriends, but Lila was horrified at the thought and did not care to participate. Now she wished she had. Since Kyla's death, Lila wished she had participated in a lot of things. The memories would have been good company.

***

The clouds had disappeared. The sun was overhead now, and she cast no shadow. She'd been walking for hours and her stomach was starting to growl. She turned and calculated the distance back, and decided to exit the beach and find a fast food place. Her legs had started to ache, and she was sweaty. She planned a dip after lunch to cool off, and an hour or two in a beach chair with her journal and a pen. Chronicling the day was a ritual, too.

As Lila trudged through the sand toward a beach exit to the boardwalk, she squinted at a shoe perched on top of one of the slats of the gate. She stood motionless, letting memories wash over her.

"Lila, look at these! They are perfect!" Lila swung around in the aisle of the shoe department of Belk's where the sisters had been shopping, and examined a pair of rainbow-colored, sequin-encrusted flats. She determined she would not blurt out her immediate thought about the shoes, which was that she would not wear them in a million years; and responded with a neutral, "Oh, wow!"

But Kyla was entranced. She referred to them as princess slippers, and wore them incessantly from the moment she plunked down her debit card.

The shoe atop the gate was the exact, same shoe. At least she thought it was.

Lila remembered the last time she'd seen that shoe. Her mother had asked her to pick out what Kyla would have wanted to wear for her funeral, and Lila had sobbed her way through selecting coffin attire for her sister. She had torn the room apart looking for Kyla's beloved princess slippers. She only found the left shoe, and didn't think her sister would have appreciated being buried in one shoe, so she had no choice but to choose another pair. Lila had carefully saved that shoe. In fact, it resided in a box containing several of Kyla's favorite things on a shelf at the top of her closet.

Lila shook her head, told herself thousands of people lost shoes on the beach every day, and this was a way to alert the owner. That was all.

But she checked the size anyway. 7B.

Kyla's size.

She wrestled with taking the shoe as a memento, or leaving it there for the owner to retrieve. The shoe was incredibly worn, so if the owner returned, would they really want it back? She sighed and decided she would think about it after lunch.

Two hours and a full stomach later, she still had not made up her mind about whether to take the shoe, but returned to the site to think about it some more. When she arrived, she was surprised to see a deeply-tanned young man with a surfboard under his arm contemplating the shoe. Lila hung back a bit, pretending to be fascinated by a sand dune; peripherally watching. He reached for the shoe and let his fingers trail over its contours, seemingly lost in thought. He bowed his head and closed his eyes for a moment, then, perhaps embarrassed, quickly glanced around to see if anyone had noticed. His gaze landed on Lila and he stared a long moment, then grinned and shrugged. Lila smiled back and walked over.

"Nice shoe," she said. "Do you know who the owner is?"

"Yeah," he said. "I do."

She raised her eyebrows at him, questioningly. He sighed, planted his surfboard in the sand, and motioned for her to join him on the boardwalk steps, a few paces away from the gate.

"Name's Chad," he said, as he sat on the steps and stretched out a hand.

"Lila," she responded; and grasped his hand.

"Y'know, I am surprised that shoe is still there," Chad said. "I put it there years ago. It belonged to a friend of mine, a girl I was dating. She's gone now."

Lila felt a chill run up her spine. She whispered, "What happened?"

Chad leaned back on his hands and turned his head toward the ocean. The waves were higher now, and the breeze had picked up. The yellow flag had been raised. "I talked her into surfing. She didn't much want to, but I'd been teaching her to surf a little, and she said okay. Waves were rough, but not too bad; really a pretty good day for the board."

He paused. Every nerve ending in Lila's body was vibrating.

"Well, she had on those shoes. Called them her princess slippers. My nickname for her was "Princess," because of those shoes. She kicked them off, grabbed my board and slid into the water, clothes and all. While she was out there, the tide came in and sucked one of her shoes off the beach. When she came back in, she found out her shoe was gone and threw a fit. A big one, right there on the beach in front of everybody. Of course, it was all my fault." He smiled at the recollection. "I was crazy about her, but she moved on, things didn't work out. Her shoe washed up on the beach a few weeks later, and I put it on the gate as a – well, I don't know – maybe I thought she might come back for it. I kind of lost track of her until I read about her funeral a few years back." He leaned toward her, a puzzled look on his face. "You look *exactly* like her!"

Lila swallowed, a tear making its way slowly down one cheek. She rose and picked up the shoe, and hugged it to her chest. Chad furrowed his brow. "Did Kyla never tell you she had a twin?" She extended her hand to him. His expression was priceless. "Let's walk," she said.

photo by Debra Eloise

The Left Shoe
by Betsy A. Riley

We had a fight and he moved out
I even helped him pack
but now I'm feeling sorry
and I'd like to have him back

So many angry words were said
I don't know what to do
then as I cleaned the closet out
I found his one left shoe

I've something that belongs to him
something he left behind
and he'll be by today at two
to hear what's on my mind

This shoe is lonely just like me
because he has its mate
but we could make a perfect pair
I hope it's not too late

Now I'm crying in the hallway
'cause I see he understands
for he's standing on my doorstep
with the right shoe in his hand

 **Regina Sokas'** articles have appeared in newspapers across the country, from the *Portland Oregonian* to the *Staten Island Advance* and the *New Orleans Times-Picayune*. The latter is particularly wonderful to say aloud. Most recently, her slightly skewed love poems were published in the April 2011 anthology *Life In Me Like Grass On Fire*. She is a Johns Hopkins-trained psychotherapist. (One word. Not two.)

Regina's entry, *"On Black Ice,"* is a drama.

photo by Tim Jones

ON BLACK ICE

by Regina Sokas

The spin ended with Sally's Buckingham Blue Evoque suddenly northbound along Route 97 and, though safe from oncoming traffic on the road's shoulder, just a kiss away from the rough-hewn wood of a telephone pole.

"I don't suppose you could keep this from your father," she blurted out, immediately regretting it.

Vivi, her fourteen-year-old daughter, didn't even bother with an answer, but continued rapidly texting. A sudden vision appeared with a far future, old, frail Vivi, staring vacantly, her sea green eyes grown rheumy, but her thumbs, those bent, arthritic thumbs, still frantically flailing, forever texting friends who were gone. Sally shook it off, glad that she wouldn't be alive to see it in person.

"My Mom just tried to kill me with her car. LOL," was the Facebook status Sally would later discover. Sally would be impersonating a teenager at the time, of course, since Vivi was willing to friend random fictional strangers but not her own mother.

Sally shivered and loosened her grip on the steering wheel. "I think we're okay. Stay put while I check." She unbuckled her seat belt and left the SUV, circling around the back. New snow shrouded the plowed mounds with clean, white beauty. No damages there.

As she neared the front of the vehicle, though, she saw a familiar glove, striped at the cuff, with an enormous pouf of knitted rosette growing out of the base of the thumb and spinning the width of the hand. "Ridiculous," Sally had pronounced at the Nordstrom counter just days ago. "Why would anyone pay nearly two hundred dollars for a glove without fingers?"

Allison, her almost neighbor, simply laughed. "Be careful about sounding old and out-of-it," she'd said. Apparently, one by-product of the new techno age was an explosion in fingerless gloves. Cold digits were much better than temporarily uncommunicative ones. Allison had waggled her own digits at Sally, then purchased a pair, just to prove that she was still hip.

Sally picked up the glove, plucking at little ice balls that clung to its surface. Vivi rolled down her window. "Can we go now? I'm going to be late," she whined. Vivi was unfamiliar with suffering in silence.

Sally ignored her, forcing herself to look more carefully at the splash of color that protruded awkwardly from the side of the snow mound. Fuchsia suede, with a burst of fur like a fringe of bangs peeping out from a snowcap. The latest in Ugg boots, not yet available in the stores stateside, picked up by Allison during a recent trip to Australia to visit her eldest, a college Junior enjoying a semester abroad in the land down under.

Sally reached out toward the boot, but encountered an unexpected solidity. The frivolous glove may be fingerless, but there was something unyielding in the boot that bore a resemblance to toes. Sally began frantically digging at the snow mound like a sort of crazed St. Bernard, managing only to dislodge the fashion-forward boot.

"Mom, is that a real foot?" Vivi leaned out of the window, holding up her new smart phone to snap a photo. "Cool," she said

Sally spun around, snatching the phone from her daughter's outstretched hand. Those abortive tennis lessons kicked in, and she swung as if acing a serve--except for the release part. You weren't supposed to let go of the racket at the end of the swing. They both watched as the phone hurtled into the distance.

***

"What the hell were you thinking? Replacing that damn phone's going to cost me a bundle." Derek jerked at his necktie, pulling it loose. He had circles under his eyes. Burning his candle too much lately.

Sally remained externally calm. "I was thinking that we didn't raise our daughter to respond to tragedy by tweeting a neighbor's fresh corpse to all her little friends."

Derek blinked and turned away. "No, no, of course not. But still . . . that was an expensive phone."

Sally was fully aware of how expensive that hated little electronic barrier had been. She swallowed her annoyance, however, washing it down with the familiar longing that always seemed to bathe her in Derek's presence.

She leaned softly into Derek's shirt back. Or nearly leaned, holding back her weight, really only inclining a single cheek in his direction, and even then not straying close enough to transfer her makeup to the starched cotton. It was more a suggestion of a lean. A whisper of body language instead of a shout. If Derek felt her behind him at all, he didn't show it but continued unbuttoning his cuffs.

As he began to shrug the shirt off, Sally noticed his slight hesitation. She waited.

"And it was definitely your friend, Allison?" he said.

"Mmmhmm," Sally confirmed as the cotton fell away from shoulders that still reflected a youth hard bought with hours at the gym.

"Damn," Derek sat on the edge of the bed, holding the shirt awkwardly. He was so rarely awkward. Sally found this slight confusion compellingly attractive. She dropped to the bed beside him. Derek didn't move away. "What do they think happened?" he asked. "How did she end up in a snow bank?"

Sally shrugged. "It was terrifying, the sight of her glove. Her boot. And then realizing that she was actually *there*. An actual human body. There. On the road. I didn't know what to do." She waited for him to reach out and comfort her.

He stood up and began draping his shirt over a chair back. "I can see that," he said. "Though I wish you had thought of a different way of expressing your shock. That was a $300 phone."

Sally sat back on the bed as if she'd been slapped, then stood abruptly. "What were the two of you talking about at the Meikeljohns' Superbowl party?" she demanded.

Derek turned toward her. "What?"

"You know what I'm talking about. I saw you two huddled together for the longest time. What was so fascinating?"

"You're really asking me this?"

"Why can't you tell me?"

"Really? A friend and neighbor of ours dies, dies in the street, on the same street I take to work every day. The same street you take Vivi to dance class. And what you're wondering about is what I was talking about with her at a party three weeks ago. You need to have a talk with that therapist of yours because she clearly isn't doing you any good."

Sally was so taken by surprise at Derek having any idea at all where Vivi's dance class was located that she found herself without words.

Derek pulled on his sweats. "I'm not doing this anymore, Sally. I'll be at the gym."

Sally stood for a very long moment, just staring at the door. She picked Derek's shirt from the chair, pushed out her lower lip in an exaggerated pout and wiped Derek's favorite shirt across her mouth, leaving a brilliant magenta streak of Chanel's La Sensuelle along the collar.

***

The girls were meeting at Panera's for lunch. Sally had deliberately picked it because it lacked a liquor license. It seemed wrong to sip cocktails with the group so soon after one of their members had died in an alcohol-related incident.

"I heard that Allison's blood alcohol level was nearly three times the legal limit," Brittany said, somewhat breathlessly, as if repeating gossip belabored her. She was young and wispy and the daughter she had in the dance team was really a step from her husband's first marriage. "I didn't think she seemed drunk, did you?"

"Extreme dieting and martinis don't mix," Marilou said. She was the fat one of the group and, therefore, tended to call most dieting extreme and then blame it for all the ills of the world. Marilou's daughter was such a stick that the others all suspected an eating disorder, though nobody said it out loud.

Sally had approached Vivi with questions of anorexia or bulimia among the dance team girls. "Gross," had been Vivi's one-word reply.

Brittany turned to Sally. "You gave her a ride home that day. Did you notice anything?"

Sally sighed deeply and then cut a small bite from her turkey and artichoke panini. She hesitated, her fork in mid-air, then signed again and set it back down. "No, I didn't notice. I just feel so terribly guilty. I should have waited until I saw her go inside. I ask myself over and over again why she wandered off."

Her friends made the appropriate soothing noises, and Sally returned to eating her lunch.

Sally left out the part about how she and Allison had stopped for 'just one more' in an attempt to get her to talk about Derek, but despite the extra martinis, Allison had revealed nothing.

She also left out the part about how she had deliberately taken Allison to the wrong house, letting her out in front of a nearly identical tasteless Italianate monstrosity just one court up from her own.

Marilou stabbed at her salad as if she hated it for not being an éclair. "No food plus alcohol. Who knows what she was thinking?"

Sally smiled a sad, little smile. "One of those times when you just wish you could read minds." The others nodded. Sally would have to have been a psychic genius to have predicted that this simple, humiliating prank of dumping Allison at the wrong address, barely a quarter mile from her own house, would somehow result in a death. Nobody could be blamed for not being a psychic.

"I hope Lizbeth keeps up with her dance. Allison was so proud of her abilities," Brittany said. "The other girls would miss her so much."

"I'm sure we can all take turns bringing her," Marilou said, her voice breaking. "Poor Lizbeth shouldn't have to pay the consequences for such a tragic mistake."

"Of course we can," Sally soothed. "Although this is also a teachable moment for our own girls. Everything has consequences," she said. "Always has. Always will."

photo by Debra Eloise

Nancy Clark Townsend was born and raised in the Inwood section of northern Manhattan, New York City, but lived most of her life in the Lower Hudson Valley of New York State. She has always shared her home with an assortment of dogs and cats, and owned and raced several harness horses. She studied Creative Writing at Empire State College, and took courses offered by "Writer's Digest". She has written several romance and suspense novels and is currently working on a sequel to her first book, ***Furred & Feathered Friends: Katrina Castaways***, which was published in February 2012. She is the editor and writer for "*Church Chatter*" a newsletter for her church, for which she creates a Bible Word Search and Bible Acrostic. She is now retired from her work as a legal and education secretary. Nancy worked with teachers to write and produce curriculum guides for elementary and high school students. In one, she re-wrote and modernized several of Aesop's Fables. Nancy belongs to two on-line writing groups – Advanced Writing Workshop and AARP's Writing Memoir.

"*The Dog and the Nike*" inspired Nancy's romantic suspense novel, ***The Witness wore Fur***.

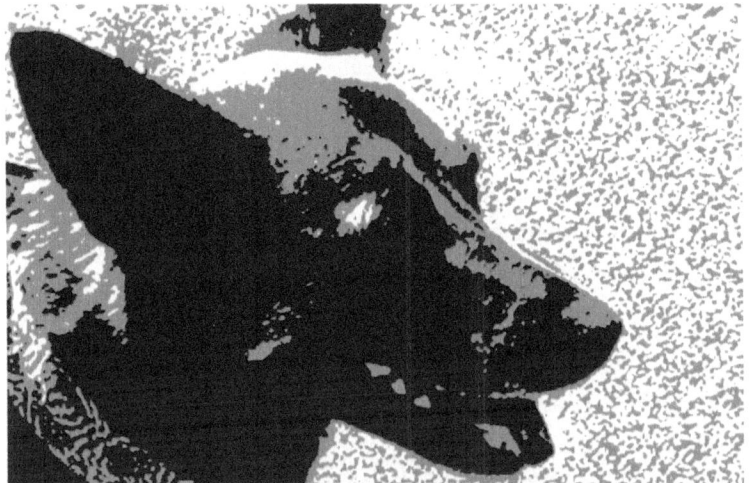

image modified by Betsy A. Riley from photo by Debra Eloise

THE DOG AND THE NIKE

by Nancy Clark Townsend

W hat was that? Wendy's eyes flew open. She could feel her heart pounding as she sat up in bed. Disoriented, she forced herself to calm down, shaking her head to clear the cobwebs in her brain.

A scream. Definitely a scream. Had she been the one who screamed while in the throes of some elusive nightmare? She had been dreaming so often lately – a symptom of a cluttered mind or anxiety or both. She didn't know which troubled her more, the vaguely disturbing dreams or the sleeplessness.

If she could only sleep through one solid night without dreaming or waking several times. How would she manage if she had to get out and go to a job every day? She knew she was fortunate that, as an author, she could work at home and set her own hours. Sighing, Wendy lay back down, but she became aware that she was listening intently, barely breathing. The scream – if indeed it had been real – had to come from the woods beyond the house.

Maybe it hadn't been real. Perhaps it was actually another noise that had penetrated her dream. An intruder trying to gain entrance? Or worse, maybe already inside? This caused her to sit up yet again and swing her legs around, toss off the quilt and sit on the side of the bed. She checked the alarm system and all the windows and doors. Everything was secure.

That was when Wendy heard the dog, and this was not a dream. It howled – a shrill, piercing sound that went right through her. Then it barked several times before she heard it yelp as if in pain. What was going on out there? The quiet of the night returned and she knew there was nothing she could do before daylight.

She climbed wearily back in bed and waited for sleep to come.

The rain that started a short while later helped lull her to sleep at last. It was midmorning when she woke. It had stopped raining and looked as if the sun was trying to break through, so after lunch Wendy went outside to skim the leaves from the in-ground pool. Suddenly she was startled by a sound and she stopped to listen. There it was again – a soft whine or whimper. She set the long-handled net down and walked out onto the lawn.

"Where are you, buddy?" she called out as she stepped down onto the lawn. "Here boy!"

She walked toward the wooden yard gate and stopped to listen again. The dog, for there was no doubt that was what she heard, whimpered again. He or she was right outside the gate. She hesitated –but the animal called once more. This time it was a very long and weak howl.

She unlocked the gate and pulled it open. The dog, a male German shepherd, lay on his right side, his nose against the gatepost. He whimpered again, and she stooped to get a closer look. He was sopping wet from being out in the rain and he shivered uncontrollably. She gasped when she saw what appeared to be several knife wounds scattered over his body. They were encrusted with drying blood. The worst gash was at the top of his left rear leg. There were two puncture wounds around his ribcage, and yet another gash on the back of his neck.

Wendy wondered how the dog had made his way out of the woods with such grave injuries.

"I won't hurt you, buddy," she said soothingly. "It'll be okay sweet boy."

He lifted his head slightly, and his tail thumped the ground weakly. He was panting heavily; his eyes were dull with shock and pain. She stroked his side, and she could feel the heat radiating from his body despite the fact that he was shivering. He was already feverish.

"Wait right there," she said.

As if he could run away. It had undoubtedly taken all his strength to reach the gate.

Wendy ran back to the house and into the kitchen. She grabbed her cell phone and while she hurried back to the dog she speed-dialed the Vinton Veterinary Clinic. Jean Vinton answered the phone.

"Jean, its Wendy Malcolm."

"Hi, Wendy. I've been meaning to call and see how you're doing."

"I'm so-so in general, but right now a badly injured stray dog has shown up by my rear gate. I can't move him to bring him in…."

"Can you tell what his injuries are?"

"He has several wounds. My guess is they are from a knife or something else that's sharp. There's a lot of drying blood, he's shivering from the wet and cold, and he's running a fever.

"I'll bring the van over and take a look at the dog. Be there in a few."

"Thanks. Just come around the back. He's by my yard gate. Should I give him water? He's panting."

"No, just let him be. If he has internal injuries the water will do more harm than good. You might saturate a washcloth in cold water and wipe his mouth – let him suck on that if he will or drip some onto his tongue. I know it's tempting, but don't try to tend to those wounds or cover him up. It's best just to let him be for the moment."

While she waited for Jean, Wendy brought a bowl of water and a washcloth outside. She sat on the grass beside the dog. He wagged his tail weakly for a moment. She took the cloth and wet it thoroughly, then began to sponge his mouth, letting water drip on his tongue. He licked at it eagerly. His eyes were crusted with mucus but she made no attempt to clean him up. His breathing was labored.

"You poor thing," she whispered. "I'll take care of you, buddy. Don't you worry."

People say such inane things to animals, as if they could understand. But she knew that dogs found comfort in gentle human voices, so she continued to talk to him. Not long after, Wendy heard the vet's van as it climbed the steep driveway, then the door slammed, and she caught sight of Jean running up the stone steps.

Jean Vinton was close to six foot tall with the body of an athlete. In fact, she had been on two Olympic women's track teams when she was young, and she still ran regularly in any marathon she could fit into her schedule. Her graying brown hair was cut short, and her brown eyes showed concern the minute she saw the dog.

"How in the world could he have gotten hurt like that?" she wondered, not expecting an answer.

Wendy told her about the howls and yelps she had heard coming from the woods during the night.

"It must have been this dog. What a bastard!" She examined the various wounds on the exposed side. "These definitely look like knife wounds."

While Wendy stroked his head, Jean took the dog's temperature.

"What a gorgeous animal," she said.

"Part shepherd do you think?"

"Personally, I'd say he's a pure bred." Jean paused. "There's nothing I can do for him here. I can't tell how deep any of these wounds are, and there are likely more on the other side. The fact that he's alive is a good sign. If an organ or artery was punctured, he'd have bled out and died before you found him."

She looked at the thermometer, then took a stethoscope and listened to his heart. Jean shone a small flashlight in his eyes.

"He's in shock from the pain and trauma, and that's more dangerous than the injuries themselves. I'm going to give him a couple of shots right off. One is an antibiotic; the other is a tranquilizer that should pretty much put him out."

"His breathing seems raspy."

"He's struggling to breathe. Could be pneumonia setting in, but this wound here," she pointed to one near his chest, "may mean a lung is punctured or bruised – hopefully the latter."

Jean had a medical kit with her and immediately went to work. Within a couple of minutes the dog was asleep.

"There's a stretcher in the car. Come help me."

"Don't worry about the bill. He may belong to someone, but I'll take care of the cost."

"As if I gave that a thought, Wendy." Jean and her husband Tony often sheltered strays, nursing them back to health and then placing them in new homes. "Pretty isolated up here for a stray unless he's come a long way or was dumped. He looks well fed, so I don't think he's been on his own long if at all."

"With what I heard last night, there's no doubt someone inflicted a lot of pain." Wendy paused. "You know, about ten minutes before that I woke up because of a scream."

"Wow," said Jean.

"The problem is, I don't know if it was real or a dream."

"Could be just coincidental. Whoever it was probably intended to kill the dog but couldn't get an accurate hit in the dark. He must have escaped and crawled here. The bastard figured he'd die, so he took off. Damn, I hate people sometimes."

Within a few minutes, they had the dog in the van.

"I'll have Tony give you a call as soon as he examines him. There's no point in your coming now."

"Okay."

***

The police searched the woods, but found nothing. No one responded to the ad she placed in the paper, so Wendy decided to keep the dog. He responded to the name Buddy, and she took that as a sign. It was touch and go for a while with his injuries, but finally he was deemed healthy enough to go back to normal activities.

Wendy welcomed his companionship while she did yard work. When the dog suddenly took off into the woods, Wendy was worried. She called to him, but he kept going. *Well,* she told herself, *you've got to let him go. He's okay now, and he wants to explore.*

It was unlikely Buddy would meet up with anything bad in the woods during the day. Night was different. However, she watched for him anxiously, and when he still wasn't back after she finished mowing the outer area, she walked to the tree line.

"Buddy!" she yelled. "Buddy!"

She heard some twigs cracking and there he was among the trees. He ran right up to her, but even before he arrived she saw he had something in his mouth. When she saw what it was, she shook her head.

"Where in the world did you get this?" she asked as he let her take a woman's filthy sneaker from his mouth.

It was a white and blue Nike with Velcro fastening and only a size six and a half. Buddy wagged his tail, ran slightly away from her, came back, and wagged his tail again. She knew what he wanted, so she threw the sneaker as far as she could toward the house. He charged after it, picked it up and tossed it in the air. They played for a while and then returned to the fenced yard. She locked the gate securely, but let him have the sneaker.

Feeling ambitious, in the afternoon she pulled weeds from the other side of the rock garden. She stared in disbelief at what the dog brought home this time – a pair of filthy, white lace panties, size 4. Even to Wendy's untrained eyes, the crotch was sliced through – not torn, but cut, with ... a knife ... or scissors, and there was a reddish brown stain. Not just a spot, but spattered. Blood?

But the police checked the woods thoroughly, she thought. The shoe she had assumed came from someone's trash – until now. The panties, *cut* panties ... a woman's sneaker. A rapist, here, in her woods? She shuddered. The night Buddy was attacked. The scream that had awakened her. It. Had. Been. Real.

With the sun still high in the sky, Wendy put on her hiking boots. The woods would darken even before the sun set beyond the Ridge, so she took a plastic flashlight lantern just in case. She opened the yard gate and Buddy pranced happily beside her. She played with him for a minute and waited. When he started for the woods, she followed.

Buddy seemed happy she was with him. He would wait for her to catch up and continue ambling along, but that he had a specific destination in mind soon became apparent.

The dog headed almost straight west to the Ridge. Soon the sheer white rock wall loomed before them, and at that point he turned north. She estimated they walked approximately another mile before he stopped, but they were still on her land. He looked at her and disappeared beneath one of the many shrubs that grew at the base of the Ridge.

Wendy called to Buddy, but he didn't return. She waited and noticed that the bush didn't move. When he first went under, the branches and leaves stirred. Now they were still. Suddenly, he barked, and the muffled sound had an echo. She called him again. The brush moved, and he reappeared. He barked at her and disappeared once more. She walked up to the mountain laurel and separated the branches, but she couldn't see anything. Buddy barked as if asking her to come to him.

Now there were butterflies in her stomach, and she hesitated. There obviously some kind of cave or small opening behind the bush. She wondered about bats or something even bigger. Wasn't spring the time when critters gave birth? But the dog couldn't be in there if it was currently inhabited as a den for a fox or other animal.

Wendy got down on her knees and pushed the branches aside, still managing to hold on to the lantern. She made her way through the thick bush and found that there was a place she could stand up. She did so and stared down at Buddy. He stood in the opening of a cave and in his mouth was a strip of dirty cloth. He relinquished it to her and she examined it. It was a piece of white blouse with two pearl-like buttons attached.

She checked out the opening. It was half her height but wide enough for even a man to get through. Heart pounding, and against her better judgment, Wendy crouched down and went inside. Here she was, acting the foolish heroine who did insanely stupid things in movies and books. Not enough light penetrated for her to see, so she flicked on the lantern. She couldn't tell how deep the cave might be. The beam didn't illuminate beyond a few feet. She heard faint fluttering noises and some peeping. Without a doubt she was disturbing resident bats.

What held her gaze was the floor of the cave. It was surprisingly level and there were bones scattered about. Comparatively intact were the remains of a rib cage and skull off to her right – part of a human skeleton; suddenly Wendy felt sick to her stomach. Near the skull was a pair of jeans. She saw crew socks and the rest of the blouse. None of the clothing was on the skeleton. If the woman, and she was certain it was a female, had been dressed when killed, wouldn't there be remnants of torn clothing from the animals that had likely devoured her remains?

The neck bone was still connected to the skull and torso. There were bunched up pieces of what looked like duct tape.

Two long bones, detached from the skeleton, were connected to hands, the wrists held together by a pair of handcuffs.

"My God," she breathed.

photo by Debra Eloise

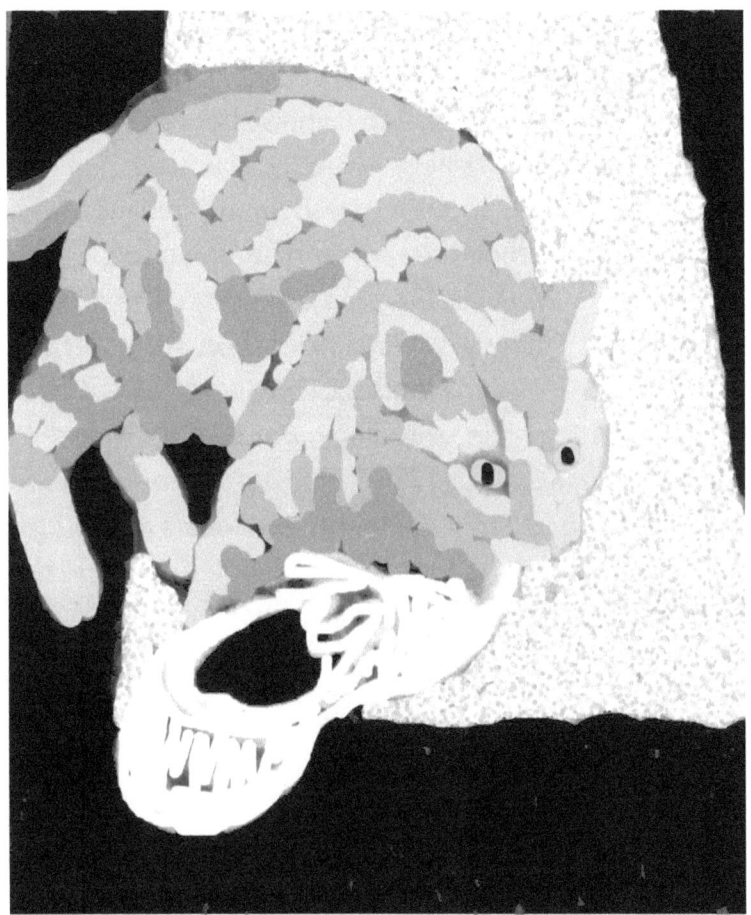

illustration by Betsy A. Riley based on photo by Karen Pao

 **Desdemona Pike** is a pen name for multi-genre author, Betsy A. Riley. As Desdemona, she writes about murders and serial killers, typically characters on the road. If you see Desdemona credited as the author, then someone is going to die. Her Works in Progress are novels ***The Scream Collector*** and ***Payback's a Bitch.*** Her short story "Second Opinion" appears in the April 2012 issue of *SNM Horror Magazine*, and in the anthology ***Bonded by Blood V***. Another story, "Curiosity Kills", will be in the ***Aspiring Writers 2012 Short Story Competition Winners Anthology***. She is a member of the Eldersburg Critique Group and the Carroll County Chapter of MWA.

Her entry is "The Hand Painted Crocs".

photo by Debra Eloise

THE HAND PAINTED CROCS
by Desdemona Pike

It was actually my girlfriend Crissy who came up with the idea. She was the one who noticed the shoes on the side of the road. I was griping about my lack of inspiration for my senior photography exhibit. True, it was still a few months away, but it would be a lot of work.

This year everyone was supposed to use a theme, sets of photographs of similar subjects. We could mix color and black & white, but all pieces had to be matted and framed, with a blurb about the subject written on cards. "Make us see your subjects in a different way," the professor had said, "make us FEEL something. Set a mood."

I was partial to decaying buildings or rusting structures, but I had to try something different. I'd already heard that Bobby was going to shoot the old railroad bridges. Lots of architectural geometry, damn. And Carl-David was shooting his grandfather's collection of old farm tools. Cynthia was shooting backstage shots at kiddy pageants. Not my thing, but she was brilliant at catching fleeting expressions. Those three were my rivals. I had to come up with something unexpected.

"Look, there's one now," Crissy said. I barely caught a glance of a shoe on the left shoulder before we were past it. "You should take photos of the shoes left on the side of the road. Seems like there's a couple of new ones every time we make this trip." The photographic supply store on campus was overpriced, so we regularly drove to the next county where there was a discount warehouse next to a mall. I could drop Crissy off to shop and take my time drooling over enlargers, lenses, and filters. I usually ended up just buying chemicals, film, and paper.

After putting my purchases in the trunk, I met up with Crissy in the food court. I must have browsed longer than I thought, because she was already waiting, sipping a milkshake. "I've decided," she said when I walked up, "Joshua, you just have to do the roadside shoes as your project. I'll be your spotter." I was skeptical, but she made me promise to try shooting the one we'd seen on the way over.

I had to admit it was more interesting than I'd thought. The shoe was a red high heel, on the shoulder next to an abandoned junkyard. I was able to get some super low angle shots with the pristine shoe backed by tangled, rusted metal seen through a chain link fence. I could already see what the finished prints would look like. They'd be killer shots.

I expected Crissy to get bored while I set up angles and exposures. I'm really a perfectionist when it comes to my art. But she had used her time at the mall to buy a book to read and some cold bottled water for the trip back to campus. When I finally wrapped the shoot and came back to the car, she presented me with a leather-bound blank book. "Remember to record the notes about the subject," she said, "you know, date and time, where you took the shot, shutter speed, all that technical stuff you'll need for the cards." She's a real gem. I would have forgotten to record the details and had to fudge the blurbs. Risky with the professor having such a sharp eye.

We found times when we both were free, and roamed the roads in the area. The best hunting was always on the highway to the next county. Usually I left the shoes exactly where i found them, but there were a couple I couldn't resist taking. One was a really distinctive cowboy boot, had to have been custom made. It was cream leather with an teal lizard inset up the side of the shaft, surrounded by echo stitching. I figured I could put a bunch of flowers in it and set it on the guestbook table at my show. Crissy volunteered to find just the right arrangement.

The other shoe I took was a child-sized croc that had been hand painted. I found it just the day before the show and had to really rush to add that one last photo. A bold daisy spread across the toe and vamp, and little ladybug plugs had been inserted in some of the ventilation holes. It was really cute. I planned to use it as a business card holder for the show.

I was excited as I hung my pieces for the show. Crissy had gotten an arrangement of Gerbera daisies that matched the daisy painted on the croc. She interspersed them with pheasant quills to echo the tall weeds that were in the background of the boot photo. My anchor pieces were the boot photo and the red heel. The center piece was the shot of the child's croc.

I had laid down on the asphalt to get that shot. The colorful shoe loomed bright and cheerful in a beam of sunlight, against a background of darkly ominous forest. The special lens I had used made the tree branches seem to be grabbing for the shoe. I thought it was my best shot ever.

The show went really well. I got lots of positive comments in my guest book, and I had to refill the business cards twice. I suspected a lot of the folks just came for the free punch and cookies, but many did seem to be carefully studying the photographs.

Near the end of the evening, my professor came up leading an elderly man in a clerical collar. "Josh, this is Father Herman, from the Unitarian Church over in the next county. He would like to talk to you about doing another exhibit." I shook hands with the minister and he explained that they had a hallway between their sanctuary and classroom where they often displayed artwork, and he'd like to have my photography exhibit displayed there. I didn't know how great that type of exposure would be for me, but the professor gave me a nod and a wink, so I agreed.

"There's just one thing," the minister said, "could you put the display up tomorrow? I hate having bare walls. I thought my secretary had arranged a new display, and she thought I had." He shook his head, "I'm afraid we're both getting old. Could you meet me there at 8 a.m. tomorrow to get set up? We have a special service later in the morning, and I'd like the exhibit up by then."

The old man looked eager, so I agreed. Because of the early morning appointment, I didn't linger with the other students to exchange congratulations over the success of the show. Crissy and I just packed up quickly, and for once left everything in the car and hit the sack.

We found a drive-thru for coffee and biscuits on the way over to the church the next morning. Father Herman met us at the driveway, where he was changing the signboard to read "Special Prayer Service for Amber Jeffers, 9 AM". He rode with us across the parking lot to show us the closest place to park for carrying stuff in.

It was a nice setup, the hallway was about the same length as the gallery space, so I was able to use the same layout. He didn't mind nail holes, and even said it was okay to put the little table with the flowers and business cards at the end of the hall.

By the time I finished measuring and hammering, that coffee wanted out. People were starting to arrive for the special service and I wanted to linger just a little to see if the photos got any notice. I made sure the photos were hung just so and dashed to the men's room, so I was down the hall when the screams started. It was a woman, screaming hysterically, "My baby, my baby!" When I made it back around the corner, I saw she was standing in front of the croc photo. A man was trying to comfort her, but he looked angry. She was actually trying to take the photo down off the wall.

Father Herman reached the couple the same time I did and asked what the problem was. The man answered, "That's Amber's shoe, the one she was wearing when she was taken."

"I'm sure many children's shoes look similar," the minister said, "It's a horrible coincidence, but it doesn't mean that this was your daughter's shoe."

"Yes, it does," the man snapped back, "my wife painted those shoes herself. There's not another pair like them. I want to know where this photographer saw that shoe." He stopped a moment to comfort his wife, "I've already called the police, Detective Sanders should be here any minute."

"Well the photos aren't going anywhere," the minister said, "why don't we go back to my study where your wife can have a seat and some privacy while we wait for the authorities to arrive." He motioned to me, "Joshua, it's best that you come too. Have your girlfriend watch over your exhibit so nobody tries to walk off with a souvenir."

It was an uncomfortable wait in Father Herman's study. The couple shared a small leather sofa, and the minister sat in a swivel chair behind his desk. That left me on a straight-backed chair in between them. I felt like I was on trial. I was almost relieved when the detective arrived, on the heels of two uniforms.

Detective Sanders introduced himself and explained he'd been working the Jeffers case. Jeffers turned out to be the name of the couple. Their little girl, Amber, had been grabbed from a day care outing a couple of days before. There had been some kind of diversion, so no one actually saw the snatch. My photo was the first solid lead they'd had.

"I need to see this photo," Sanders said, "and hear any info you have about when and where it was taken." He cast a stern look at the minister and the Jeffers, "I think it's best if all of you stay here and I'll let, Josh? is it? show me the photo." He posted one of the uniforms at the door of the study so the Jeffers would not be disturbed. The other trailed us as we walked back to the hallway.

"Uh, I have complete notes on when and where all my photos were taken," I said, "will that help?" The detective nodded. "And, I actually have the shoe, too." I gulped, "it was cute, so I took it to put my cards in."

Sanders grabbed my arm, "You have the actual shoe? Who all has handled it since you found it?"

"Just Crissy and me, I guess," I said, "unless any of the folks at the exhibit last night picked it up to look at." Sure enough, when we got to the hallway, a woman was holding the croc and tilting it for a better look.

"Put that down!" Sanders ordered, startling her, and half the building, judging by how many people jumped. He ordered the hallway cleared. Some folks went into the sanctuary, but others went outside and pulled out cell phones. Sanders told the uniform to hold that woman for fingerprinting and asked Crissy if anyone else had picked up the shoe.

"Just that lady today," she said, "and there was one man last night -- it was while you were getting punch, Josh." Sanders asked if we had washed the shoe or done anything else that might destroy trace evidence. "I dusted it a little," Crissy said, "but I used one of those fluffy fiber dusters, not a cloth."

Sanders lifted the shoe into an evidence bag using his pen, then asked me to show him my notes about when and where it was taken. "Hmm, that's the opposite side of town from where everyone has been searching," the detective said, almost to himself. "Do you think you could find the exact spot again?" I looked at Crissy, my human GPS. She nodded.

Soon there were more cops than I thought a town that size would even have, filling the parking lot. Sanders took Crissy and me in his unmarked. He brought along the photo for reference. Crissy pointed out the spot, and we pulled over. Some of the cops stopped behind us, and some went on a ways ahead. I explained that I had lain on the asphalt to get the shot, and pointed out particular branches that matched the photograph as proof this was where we found the shoe.

Sanders asked us to sit in the car while they did a quick search. He said his air conditioning wasn't working, so we'd be more comfortable in one of the squad cars. Yeah, right, locked in the back of one of the squad cars. Nobody was saying it, but I knew we were suspects. Crissy looked about ready to cry, so I held her hand and we just sat quietly

I could see some of the officers slowly entering the woods, spaced apart in a line. Others paced the shoulder, sometimes pausing to glare at us. Detective Sanders remained by his car, talking on a cell phone. Suddenly there was a big commotion, some men ran out of the woods and others ran in, carrying what looked like giant gym bags.

When an ambulance screamed up and EMTs followed another uniform into the woods at a trot, we crossed our fingers for little Amber. They didn't choose to enlighten us. Instead a uniform came and drove us to the police station, where we were fingerprinted and swabbed for DNA. Then they put us in separate interrogation rooms. I was worried about Crissy. I saw the tears rolling slowly down her cheeks as they were taking her fingerprints.

After what seemed like forever, a stocky man in a bad suit came in, introducing himself as Detective Templeton. After some basics, he asked me for alibis. Of course he didn't call it that, he asked me where I was at several dates and times. All of the times fell within my course schedule, so I could provide solid proof from professors and students that I was in class, not out kidnapping little girls.

Templeton left without a word. There was nothing productive I could do, so I laid my head on the table and slept. It was Sanders that woke me up, Templeton was standing behind him. "You are very lucky, Joshua," Sanders said, " you are, apparently, a memorable person. We were able to confirm your alibis with your professors and several students. You are cleared as a suspect in the Amber Jeffers kidnapping."

"But those other photos of yours?" Templeton said, "some of them match other missing persons."

"So, we need you to show us exactly where you found the shoes in some of the other photos," Sanders added.

"No problem," I said, relieved, "I'm glad to help. I have my notes and Crissy has great spatial memory -- I call her my human GPS. I may get you to a approximate area, but she can pinpoint the exact spot."

The two detectives exchanged meaningful looks, then Sanders spoke up, "Miss Hamilton's alibis do not check out. For now she must remain in custody."

"We found little Amber about fifty yards in from where you found the shoe," Sanders said. "She had been locked in a dog crate, with a gallon of water and a package of hot dog buns."

"The kidnapper took photos of Amber crying," Templeton snapped, "and came back each day to take more photos."

"Amber is very young, and severely dehydrated and disoriented," Sanders said, "But she was able to tell us one thing. The kidnapper is female."

photo by Debra Eloise

 **Joelle Jarvis** lives with her husband and four children in Carroll County, Maryland. She has been published in *Pen in Hand.* Since graduating from the University of Maryland with a B.S. in Architecture, she has been working on a trilogy of historical fiction set in ancient Pompeii. A website is forthcoming. Joelle is a member of the Eldersburg Critique group and currently serves as the treasurer for the Carroll County Chapter of the Maryland Writer's Association (MWA).

Joelle's entry, *"Out of Place,"* is a satire that points an ironic finger at the human tendency to trivialize.

photo by Debra Eloise

OUT OF PLACE
by Joelle Jarvis

I don't like to talk to people. That's why I waited a whole day plus twenty hours and nine minutes before I called the police. Two policemen came to my house on a Friday and I told them about the orange flip-flop with the white daisy. They did not seem interested.

My mama apologized and said, "I'm sorry… he's special."

Being 'special' is supposed to mean that you see the world differently from everyone else. But it really means that people don't have to listen to you.

I live with just my mama in a cabin in Maine. There is a short path through the woods behind our house that dumps out onto the Appalachian Trail. It was the third week in September and I like to go there and watch the hikers at this time of year, because the leaves are golden and when they fall the trail is like the yellow brick road from the Wizard of Oz.

Sometimes the rotten acorns make a popping noise beneath the feet of the local joggers. I like that.

But on September twenty-second, I saw the orange flip-flop there, next to the trail. It was by itself. It had a white plastic daisy on it and polka dots that were faded in the ball of the foot and heel places. It was a left shoe, with no right one in sight. I looked.

The policemen said it probably fell out of someone's backpack and they seemed content to let that be. Mama says the policemen are too busy to perform 'lost and found' duties for flip-flops. But that night, in bed, I couldn't stop thinking about it.

The morning after the policemen left, I had French toast because it was Saturday. When I was finished, I put my coat on and walked to the trail. There was frost on the ground that cracked like eggshells beneath my feet. The flip-flop was still there. A family of four, laden with supplies, hiked by and did not look at it. Perhaps they think like the police – that it just fell out of someone's backpack. But people don't bring flip-flops to Maine at this time of year. That would be dumb. I crept closer.

I know better than to touch strange objects so I took up a stick and turned the shoe over. There was a number seven stamped on the bottom and below that a symbol of a fish in blue with the word 'Bluefish' below that.

That night I went online. My mama says I can navigate the web better than anyone she knows. It is much better than having to ask a librarian for help. I looked up 'Bluefish'. I got lots of hits but the most promising was a link to a beach attire shop in South Carolina. When I clicked on the tab for shoes, a picture of the orange flip-flop with the white daisy came up. Only there were two of them in the picture – a pair. Under the photo, the caption read: *Fun-in-the-Sun flip-flop available July and*

August only. Hurry. Supplies limited. Lucky for me the website had not been updated recently.

I am not a good judge of people, but it seemed logical to me that someone with a Fun-in-the-Sun flip-flop would not want to leave just one behind. That would not be fun. Surely that person would have come back to look for it by now - unless that person could not come back because they were dead or kidnapped.

I searched the South Carolina databases for missing persons since July. There were two girls, ages nine and seventeen, and there was one boy, age eleven. Boys do not wear orange flip-flops with white daisies on them. That would be weird. And a size seven shoe would be too large for the foot of a nine-year old. So I googled the name of the seventeen-year-old: Lexi Tanger.

I was surprised to see she had a website. She was a gymnast looking for a college scholarship. She had black skin and curly hair, and really big eyes, and a diamond in her navel. She did not have Fun-in-the-Sun flip-flops on in any of the pictures, but in one of the photos I saw something I recognized.

The photo was taken around Easter time. Lexi was making the peace sign with one hand and with the other she was holding the handle of a basket of colored eggs. Attached to the belt loop of her cut-off jeans was a keychain. There was a logo of a black bear on a wooden disc and below it dangled a green spray-painted pinecone. Mr. Walters at the country store makes those and sells them to tourists. I printed the picture of Lexi.

The next day was Sunday, which means church with mama in the morning. Mr. Walters attends our church so after the service I showed him the picture of Lexi Tanger. Mama apologized for me being special again and told Mr. Walters I was working on some new project.

"I don't recognize the girl," Mr. Walters said. "But just before Easter I sold several dozen of these key chains to Coach Martin in town. He wanted to give them as souvenirs to the girls from out of town who were coming to his competition."

I didn't know Coach Martin, but Mr. Walters told me where to find him. After mama's chicken and rice and gravy dinner, I rode my bike there. The place was a warehouse with 'Starlight Tumblers' painted on the front. All the doors were locked and no one answered when I knocked. But when I yelled, I heard someone yell back – faintly. It took me a moment to realize the sound had not come from the warehouse but from a shed behind the warehouse. I knew to listen when the cars were not passing by on the road.

The shed was set back in the trees. When I got close I could hear someone inside calling for help. The shed was locked and the only windows were narrow rectangles at the very top. I had to find a drum that was a trashcan and turn it down-side-up and push it over to the window so I could climb on top and see inside.

The light in that place was only gray, but I could still see Lexi, sitting on the floor, all tied up. She had a scarf tied around her mouth but I could still hear her cries because I have good ears. Near the door was an orange flip-flop with a white daisy.

"Get the police!" Lexi said. I think she was crying and she couldn't speak well with that scarf in her mouth.

But I shook my head. "I already tried that. They didn't believe me. But I know where your other flip-flop is."

I dropped to the ground and raced on my bike back to the trail behind my house. Now that Lexi wasn't a stranger anymore I could touch her flip-flop. I thought about how happy she was going to be to have her Fun-in-the-Sun flip-flop back! Orange flip-flops with white daisies on them do not belong by the side of a trail by themselves.

photo by Debra Eloise

 **Delfina Hex** is a pen name of a multi genre author. Delfina is credited for works that dip into the paranormal, without involving physical monsters, so no zombies or vampires (those she leaves to her sister Cassandra Hex). But sentient vegetation, vindictive winds, and carnivorous canyons are fair game. Her work definitely tends towards the dark side, often into the horror genre.

Her entries, *"The Kudzu Conspiracy"* and *"Slot Canyon Rules"* are more to the paranormal side of fantasy, while *"The Glass Slipper Arrangement"* is more simple fantasy.

image modified by Betsy A. Riley

THE KUDZU CONSPIRACY
by Delfina Hex

The bus split open like a peapod, scattering passengers and their belongings along the roadway. Becky flew through the air, the only passenger not surprised by the turn of events.

She had been standing in the aisle outside the small toilet when she saw the attackers. A jeep following the bus held men dressed in camouflage with streaks of paint on their faces. When she saw one raise a rocket launcher to his shoulder and aim at the bus, she ran towards the front.

Perhaps that was why she was flung so much farther than the others when the bus exploded. She landed in the middle of the kudzu that draped the roadside in a lacy blanket of green.

Many of the passengers were still strapped in their seats, trapped in the smoldering bus. Those spilled onto the roadway lay in pools of blood from compound fractures and cuts caused by flying glass and ripped sheet metal.

Becky lay suspended in a hammock of vines, giving her a bird's eye view of the wreckage. She watched in disbelief as the men in camouflage began to execute the wounded passengers. These are terrorists, she thought. They were killing men, women, and children without pause. She shuddered at the sound of their screams. Worse, the men appeared to be Americans--they even had American flag patches on their sleeves.

Seeing the gunmen were sparing no one, Becky wormed her way down into the kudzu. It was difficult going; she was certain her right leg was broken, and her left knee was wrenched badly. Her left shoe was missing. She'd seen the red ballet flat sitting conspicuously on the edge of the pavement before she ducked her head under the kudzu vines. Just her luck to lose the shoe off her less injured leg. The right shoe would do her no good.

The ground under the kudzu sloped, so she could still glimpse the roadway between the leaves. The gunmen were swarming the crash scene. She began to worry about that left shoe. It was so far away from the rest of the wreckage that it might start the terrorists looking for a person flung that far.

She pulled her black jacket closed, to hide the red shell she wore underneath. She took off her right shoe and buried it in the loose drift that had accumulated under the ceiling of vines. If only there was some way to retrieve that left shoe.

She closed her eyes tight and wished with all her might, unconsciously clasping a thick trunk where the vine rooted in the earth. A wind seemed to stir through the vines and she felt the canopy shake. She heard yelling and more shots, but when she opened her eyes, the tell tale shoe was hidden by a loop of vines that had flopped onto the pavement.

The undulation of the vines was hypnotic, so she drifted into restless sleep. When she woke, the terrorists were gone and the bus was reduced to a charred hulk.

She felt the tendril of a vine brush against her bare foot and looked down to see her missing shoe.

PHOTO BY DEBRA ELOISE MODIFIED BY BETSY A. RILEY

SLOT CANYON RULES
by Delfina Hex

Roxanne Chandler was determined to get the best photos possible of the new slot canyon she had heard about. She wanted photos that would make those taken last year by Sylvia Martin look sick. Roxanne had been on the same photo safari, it was pure dumb luck that Sylvia was in position to shoot when the hummingbird darted into view. So Sylvia claimed the blue ribbon, breaking Roxanne's three year streak.

That was not going to happen again. Roxanne had put feelers out, so she was the first to hear about the new slot canyon tour. These canyons reportedly had some really unusual formations, a type of life-size petroglyph. The tribe considered the formations sacred, so no photography was allowed. That would be no problem for Roxanne. She had the latest in micro-miniature digital cameras stashed in her brassiere.

She had done a dry run with the hidden cameras, taking shots of the eighth-century icons in the local Greek Orthodox

Church, another organization that banned photography. She couldn't exhibit those in the local contest, but they might be her chance to finally get some of her photos published internationally.

Roxanne's sources said that the tribe that owned the land considered the tour of the canyon to be a sacred ritual, and required certain ceremonies before access. She had dressed carefully, in a demure khaki safari suit. She left off her usual jewelry and makeup. She remembered other religious sites requiring visitors to don felt scuffs to protect their surfaces. She hated wearing public shoes, so she indulged in a pair of chamois moccasins.

Roxanne was surprised to see a half dozen cars already parked at the designated spot. The trail was marked with a simple arrow. The tribe was making sure the people coming to view the canyon were committed. It was almost a mile to the open-sided hogan that marked the entrance to the canyon. She knew she was on time, so the others must have come early. They were all sitting cross-legged under the dubious shade of the brush roof.

The young shaman started the ceremony the minute Roxanne took her seat on the back row. He began by circling the group with a sage smudge. He then had each person in turn come to the front and toss a pinch of cornmeal in each of the cardinal directions, rotating clockwise. This was repeated with four pinches of loose tobacco. He explained that this was both payment to the gods for allowing them access to the sacred place, but also a prayer for their protection while inside the underworld.

The shaman handed each of them a simple woven shoulder bag, holding a pair of moccasins and a bottle of water. He took a bag for himself as he led them to the ladder.

Removing his own desert boots, he donned the pair of moccasins from the bag. He placed his left boot beside the trail, and the right boot in the shoulder bag. He explained that the shoe left behind would call to the shoe they carried in the bag, to help them find their way back safely from the underworld. The shoes would also serve as a sign to the gods and to his tribe of how many people were inside.

Roxanne hung back so that she was the last to descend. She scoffed at the line of single shoes. She descended the ladder carefully, hoping the shaman would not notice that she still had on her own shoes. She stifled a gasp when she reached the bottom. The striations of cream, ocher, and rust were more vivid than any she had seen in Antelope canyon. As the shaman led the group around a corner, she hung back to get a shot of the primitive ladder framed by the glowing colors.

Around the corner was the first petroglyph. It was of a coyote, life size, low on the wall. It didn't have the typical, stylized black outline of others she had seen. It was a solid dark brown silhouette. The shaman identified the image as "unlucky coyote". Three of the tour group knelt, murmuring some chant. The shaman led them on through a complex series of turns to the next petroglyph. This silhouette looked like a man scaling the side wall. The shaman identified it as "stubborn man". The same three knelt and chanted.

Roxanne sat down cross-legged and pretended to meditate. As soon as the group moved on, she'd get her shots and then follow. This image was so striking that she took several shots. When she hurried around the corner after the group, they were out of sight. The canyon split into three branches. The sand on the floor of the left branch looked more disturbed, so she chose to follow that one. There were more animal petroglyphs in this branch, so she happily snapped away. There was one of a bird, so large it must be an eagle. She wondered what stupid name the shaman would have for that one -- downward facing bird? The detail was amazing, she could almost swear there were real feathers in the wings.

Roxanne made sure her cameras were hidden securely and took a deep swig of her water. It seemed to be getting hotter in here, even though it was getting darker. For the first time she noticed water marks high on the walls. Although she knew that canyons were usually carved by water, she'd never thought about them still being subject to floods. She tried to recall the weather forecast and wondered if thunder would be audible at this depth.

Seized by a sudden sense of panic, Roxanne decided to retrace her steps back to the ladder. She counted the turns, but there was no "stubborn man" petroglyph. She backed up and took a different turn. Still no sign of the group, or of the ladder. The walls seemed to be closing in on her, more and more. She could feel her heart racing and sweat dripping down her back. She swallowed her pride and shouted for help. There was no answer, but she heard a faint rumbling--was that thunder?

Roxanne tried to run, but the canyon had gotten so narrow she had to flatten herself against the wall and edge sideways. The walls continued to close, pressing until her bodily fluids soaked into the sandstone, forming an image that the shaman would dub "deceitful woman" for future tours.

collage by Betsy Riley from photos by Debra Eloise

THE GLASS SLIPPER

by Betsy A. Riley

I do NOT see the attraction of glass slippers. Smarty-pants Mellisande over there, who claims she's my fairy godmother, gave me a pair, so I know what I'm talking about. Even when the pair is magically created to fit your feet perfectly, they're still . . . glass. The soles are slippery and don't flex at all, making them terrible for dancing. Thank goodness they have a peep toe cutout or they'd fill up with sweat, because-- Glass. Doesn't. Breathe. And though Mellisande tells me I have lovely feet, I don't think they're so lovely that I want the sight of my squashed together toes exposed to everyone at the ball. So the first thing I did when the coach disintegrated was toss the stupid slippers. Mellisande managed to grab one out of the air, but the other went a satisfying distance along the roadway.

Of course that left me limping along barefoot in the middle of the night, in a gown made of gossamer and moonlight. I suppose you think that sounds beautiful and ethereal. I'll let you in on a little secret: there is no warmth to gossamer and moonlight. The wind goes right through it. And if you look at just the right angle you can see all my charms -- complete with goose bumps. With my luck, the gown will disintegrate like the coach and leave me starkers.

Mellisande is ignoring my complaints and just floating along above my head, humming in that annoying way she has. What I want to know is, if she has all that magic, why can't she conjure up something practical? Some nice sturdy walking shoes and a warm cloak would be nice. For that matter, a nice cup of hot tea would be most welcome too. But no, she conjures up another wreath of flowers for my hair and a small flock of birds to flutter along chirping the same stupid tune that she hums. She was supposed to be rescuing me, but here I was, hiking back to my grim existence as a menial laborer in what was once my ancestral home.

Mellisande keeps assuring me that she has a plan, and that my prince will come. He'll come searching for me and will use the glass slipper to find his elusive dance partner, and make her his bride. Frankly, if he's that naive, I don't know if I want to marry him. It was a masked ball, so he never saw my full face-- for all he knows, I might have a giant wart on my nose. Of course everyone has seen his face, and he is quite handsome, but looks aren't everything.

While we danced, he talked about his plans for the kingdom, and they were worthy plans. But he never asked for my opinion, in fact he never asked me anything. So he never even heard my voice except for a murmured ,"yes, your majesty" when he invited me to dance. I know it couldn't have been the dancing, because those darned glass slippers had me sliding all over the place.

In fact, the only reason I could think of that would make him keen to find me was the glimpse he undoubtedly got of my charms through that gossamer and moonlight gown. Yes, I just bet he was eager to see more of me. Especially compared to all those dainty ladies at the ball, with their boyish figures and delicate natures. But I bet he could pass me on the street and not recognize me. Without the fancy gown, upswept hair, lace mask, and trimmings, he'd just see Ash Elizabeth, or Asheliz as Stepmother and her daughters have come to call me for short. He'd see a servant girl with bare feet, smudges on her face, and her back bent under sacks of potatoes or turnips.

I heard hoof beats coming up the road behind me, and tried to scramble over the verge to hide. Mellisande chose that moment to swirl the flock of birds into my face, causing me to lose my balance and fall flat on my back. "He found the slipper you threw," she whispered, "this is your moment." She dropped the slipper's mate in my lap and disappeared, just as the gossamer and moonlight gown dissolved away.

The prince dismounted and bowed, "Milady, if I might confirm your identity by trying on this slipper?" Lifting my foot to place the slipper on it gave him a view clear to midnight, which he pretended to ignore. Then he took the other slipper from my lap, none too careful about where his fingers brushed, and placed it on the other foot. I guess he approved of the view, because he drew me to my feet and kissed me. He eventually wrapped his cloak around me when we headed back to the palace. Maybe he was naive, but at least he was kind. And he was definitely a good kisser. The more I thought about it, lazing around the palace beat the heck out of digging potatoes.

I whispered a silent 'thank you' to Mellisande, and smiled, thinking just how pissed Stepmother would be when no one brought in her morning tea.

photo by Debra Eloise

photo by Debra Eloise

 **Joshua Williams** was born and lives in Central Pennsylvania. He is a full-time high school student with high aspirations of becoming an author. He enjoys writing short stories of any genre along with poetry. Whenever Joshua is not busy with schoolwork or writing, he enjoys reading or playing video games. His contribution to this anthology will be his first published story. He has been a part of *Et Cetera*, the literature and art magazine at his school, as well as a member of the National Art Honor Society.

Joshua's entry, *"The Shoe of Fate,"* is a modern fairy tale.

photo by Debra Eloise

THE SHOE OF FATE
by Joshua Williams

*D*amn, the third job turn down in two weeks. At this rate everyone has a right to call me a bum and scream angrily at me. England was supposed to be the place for me to 'rediscover' myself and start an entirely new, hopefully better, life. Now I'm stuck with hardly any cash, A single friend, and not a single achievement to my name. I should have just stayed in good old America, at least there I felt at home; I had people I could have bunked with for a while. Here, I'm just a stray dog looking for a treat in a city of cats.

Sebastian walked along a muddy street on the decaying side of Burkshire. A ubiquitous, thick fog had rolled in, making visibility elusive for those walking or driving. He had his gaze cast downward while his brain cycled a thousand times a minute, spewing negative thoughts about his recent rejections. He felt something strike his shoulder. That caused him to spin and look at a man in a suit rushing by him.

"Watch where you're going, you bloody waste." The man half shouted with a look of disgust.

You don't know the half of it, you jackass. Sebastian walked even faster with his hands clenched tight in the pockets of his sports jacket. He brought his head up to make sure no one else was careening towards him. The sidewalk transformed into a small ramp leading towards the road. He tripped on something resting in the mud at the base of the cement. Sebastian bent quickly and picked up the odd, mud-coated object. With a shrug he held it away from his body and continued walking parallel to the street on the next stretch of sidewalk.

He walked quickly through the monolithic cloud of fog until he reached the alley he had been seeking. He quickly side-stepped to enter the narrow space between two slabs of stone. The walls formed a seemingly endless hall, with what lay at the end visible to outsiders only by imagination (though Sebastian sadly knew what was there). He saw to his left against the wall an old man who had clearly seen better days.

"Hiya Henry, get anything good today?"

The man looked up at him with ice blue eyes that had not seen anything for years. He had told Sebastian he lost them during his factory days, when acid had been sprayed into his eyes. Ever since, they were nothing more than scarred bulbs. "Heya there Sebastian! Nuttin' much today, sadly. By God's grace, if this don't get much better, I'ma be kicking up begging wit me feet." Henry let out a faint chuckle before erupting into a nasty fit of coughing, caused by working in the very same factory. "How 'bout yourself Sebastian? Find any buried goodies?" The tone the man changed to was enough to mollify an angry person, and to cause a calm person to nearly break into tears; it was what made him a great beggar.

"Not much today. Got denied another job. I swear it's because I'm a goddamned American."

"Welcome to the ol' country my friend." At this Henry had another coughing fit and then rested back, as he had done many times, signaling that the conversation was finished.

Oh my dear friend. Someday I'll get you out of this rut. I'll get us both out.

Sebastian continued the trek down the alley, passing only one other man. He had seen the man before, but he had never bothered to talk with him. He reached his small alcove of blankets and cardboard located against the large stone wall that truncated the long passage. He thumped down roughly on the small patch littered with moldy bits of cardboard and dirtied blankets, that had warmed many people in their days.

He set the muddied object down on the heavily shadowed, dampened dirt. He picked up a tattered piece of yellowed cloth and began wiping off the mud-obscured object. The more he wiped away of the dark brown sludge, the more he began to realize what was being uncovered in front of him. He became shocked by how odd an object it was to come across in the streets of the poor district. A simple, yet elegant, carving of a shoe.

Of all the things I thought I would find, and that I have found, never did I dream I would find something this fancy.

He held an only slightly mud-coated black carving of an ostentatious dress shoe. The weight of the shoe was enough to confirm its potential value, even to the uneducated eye of Sebastian. The shoe had a slight gleam to it despite the gloom of the alley and the gritty coverage of mud. Sebastian's eyes also let off their own gleam, when he discovered miscellaneous gems decorating the shoe.

Now to whom exactly could you belong to my precious. Better yet, how much money can I gain for you at a nice little shop?

He turned the shoe thrice over in his hands examining every intricate detail of its structure. He looked inside and discovered neat writing on an inner label. After wiping off some of the muck covering the words, Sebastian could barely decipher what was scrawled inside: *Property of the Man of Masks.*

What the hell could that mean? I suppose a simple name or address would have been to mainstream for the uppity bastard that owned a piece of this quality. Screw him then, this baby is going to the nearest pawn shop come morning.

Sebastian turned over and tucked the shoe under the edge of the thickest blanket before letting the darkness of sleep overtake him. He thought one last time about this shoe the color of midnight, before he could officially greet the silence.

He had several nightmares during his slumber. Each revolved around the one shoe he had just discovered. In each, it either disappeared or was stolen before he could do anything of importance with it. In each, the shoe seemed to hold power over him, sending him away long enough for it to vanish, forcing him to go wandering after it, like a toddler who could not find its mother.

He awoke when the sun came out, only a few hours later, but it seemed like a decade. His hand was tightly gripped around the arch of the shoe, his knuckles turning as white as a corpse. His heart was racing, and his breathing came quick and shallow. He turned himself towards the entrance of the alley, which seemed to glow as the end of a long tunnel might. He saw Henry sitting up near the mouth and decided to go get what cash he could for the carved shoe.

He picked it up, along with a small apple stolen for his breakfast. He briskly walked towards the entrance, but was startled by a sudden voice.

"Sebastian. What did you find yesterday? I bet you're holding it right now." Henry had his eyes fixed on the ground, and Sebastian saw no reason not to tell the man about the small fortune he might acquire in the near future.

"I found a carving of a shoe."

"A carving? Of what value ? I heard you speaking in your sleep. You also rustled a good bit. I figured you must have found something interesting yesterday."

"Sorry to have woken you. It's a very good carving, of a very fancy shoe. High quality and decorated with a few gems. I'm going to take it and get however much money I can."

"Is there a name on it anywhere? Most people don't leave such nice decorations lying in the gutter."

"It just says *Property of the Man of Masks*. Whatever the hell rich idiot decided to write that. Oh well, my money now."

"I know someone who may be that very man. Well, I don't know him personally, but I know of a man referred to by that title."

"Really? Well it looks as if he lost his carving of a most elegant shoe. Time for those up above to help those down below I suppose."

"It would be worth money lad, but don't let this city ruin you like it has me. Fate and Karma are two cruel beings. Yet they can be loving. They rest heavily on those who choose a rough course."

"What? Are you going insane on me old man?" Sebastian let out a nervous cough that he meant to be a laugh.

"No time for laughing, Sebastian. I let my greed get the best of me over my life. Now look where I am. Karma affects

Fate, and when you operate with inferior intentions, Karma gets angry. And when Karma gets angry, Fate is the one who deals out the punishment. Make your decision on what you think is right lad."

"Wouldn't the money be better? It can help both of us. Why should I give a rich man back a treasure he was careless enough to lose?"

"Sometimes 'tis better to have a clean conscience and soul, rather than a full belly or shelter. You're your own person lad; do as you please. You don't have to take advice from a blind, old fool."

"Where could I find this man?"

"As far as I know, he lives in a rather grand manor house about a mile east of town. Head directly east, you should see it."

"Thanks Henry. Maybe it is better to return it, and be the better person. But wouldn't the money benefit us both far more than him?"

"It would. But I've learned something, sonny: when you live purely off money, you find things get taken away far too quickly, and after so long, no money can bring happiness."

Sebastian had no response, but one was not needed. Henry leaned back and once again ended the conversation. Sebastian looked down at the valuable object once more before making up his mind. He accelerated out of the alley and picked up his pace as he headed east alongside the road he had traveled the night before.

He felt a sense of bitter disappointment, but at the same time he knew that Henry would be prouder of him now than he ever had been.

What the hell am I doing?! I have the opportunity to get enough money to feed us for days, maybe even weeks! But there's Henry. If I don't trust him, then I truly have become soulless. Maybe some divine being will smile on me for this act. If not then I'll die, as a regretful, starving man.

Sebastian walked along the road, and eventually slightly off the road, as he began to traverse the land on the outskirts of the town. He kept his constant pace for a good while, until he saw a stone manor home erected on a short hill, not far from the road. He worked his way through the lush, green fields until he arrived at the base of a short flight of cobblestone steps leading up to a wooden door nearly eight feet tall, composed solely of cherry wood with a superfluous amount of intricate metal. .

He let his anger, at seeing a door worth more money than he could fathom, dissipate before grasping the large iron ring hanging in the middle of the door and slamming it down several times with thunderous bangs. He heard the sound of something falling inside, but realized there were no footsteps echoing towards the entryway.

A thin voice from within uttered something incomprehensible to Sebastian until he listened more closely, "It's open, my dear fellow."

Sebastian gently pushed on the heavy door and it creaked inward. He stepped in and was bombarded by the comforting smells of cheese, wine, old books, and tobacco. He continued in, to a foyer with a jeweled chandelier, and followed the slight shuffling sounds he heard farther in. He went down a short hall lit by electronic torches held by detailed carvings of hands. The hall ended in a large semi-circular library.

Bookcases reached into the air, for what Sebastian guessed to be thirty feet, and each was filled with old leather-bound novels. Although lit chandeliers hung from the ceiling, most of the lighting came from lights placed periodically along the walls. Extraordinary furniture of Victorian influence scattered the room, including desks cluttered with books and writing tools. In the middle of the room sat a short fellow with wispy white hair.

"Please, have a seat. It is rare that I get a visitor now-a-days."

"This is quite an impressive library. It must take up most of your home." Sebastian let his eyes wander all over the palace of words, before settling down in a wooden chair across from the slightly smiling man in the tuxedo.

"It takes up a good bit, but not enough to truly matter. Besides, it is full of books; there is no better way to fill a room."

"That I agree with. Now, are you the 'Man of Masks'?"

The man let out a surprised bit of laughter before answering the inquiry. "Yes, yes I am. They began to call me that during my younger days, when I hosted several dozen masquerade balls. How did you learn of that, though? I have not hosted such an event in many a year?"

"I found it on this shoe." Sebastian held up the now mostly cleaned carving, and saw a pleasant gleam appear in the man's eyes.

"Well, well, well. I suppose I owe an explanation, and an introduction. My name is Lorrie Davidson, owner of this fine estate, and, in order to completely explain the footwear, I must inform you I am near death due to cancer."

"Oh I'm so sor-"

"Don't interrupt, it isn't polite. Now, the shoe. I have no heirs, and I don't trust my things to a corrupt bank. I put that shoe there hoping someone might be generous enough to return it, though I imagine you had conflicting thoughts, yes?"

"Yes."

"As is expected. By the looks of you, no offense meant of course, you need money quite badly, yet you brought me the shoe. Why?"

"I do need money, but my closest friend told me that in the end Karma and Fate are more important. I trust his wisdom, though it seems like a fantasy to me."

"Ah, your friend is wise beyond mortal bounds. For he is right. You listened to his advice, therefore you are humble. You brought me the shoe, instead of selling it, therefore you have a desire to do good. And here is your fate: to inherit my fortune."

"What?!" Sebastian felt his head begin to swim and the world turn fuzzy.

"Yes. You show respectable attributes, all that I desire in an heir. I trust my fortune to no random devil of greed, and therefore, it shall belong to you upon my death."

"By God, I don't know what to say."

"How about your name?"

"Sebastian Trom."

"How peculiar, and you are an American none-the-less. I can tell by your still present accent. But you are what I seek, so therefore, you are now the recipient of my fortune. Treat it well, and just remember to keep those respectable attributes."

"Thank you. Thank you so much, but is it all that easy?"

"Yes. Be magnanimous, and fortune will always find you. Do malicious acts, and vengeance will seek you."

"Thank you so much. I have to go tell my friend. I can finally give him happiness in what are surely his last years."

"Right there you display a gracious heart tantamount to a saint's. Go. Return when you find your friend; you can stay here until I pass, which will be soon." The man let a smile show and then leaned back in the same fashion that Henry did.

Sebastian quickly got up and sped out of the house. He ran as fast as his under-nourished body could take him. He got to the sidewalk beside the street and slowed to a quick walk.

"Henry! Henry!" Sebastian entered the alley and saw Henry was slumped against the wall. Before he could speak, the man he had never talked to spoke to him.

"He passed a short while ago. I'm sorry friend. He just said to tell you one thing: 'Let fate guide you, and when the time comes, leave your own version of a lost shoe, to help someone else discover their heart."

Sebastian felt tears approaching, but he went to the manor house with Henry's body. There he buried Henry and lived out his life. Every year he held a masquerade in memory of his closest, and only, true friend. He kept the midnight-colored shoe on the mantel above his fireplace, to always remember his friend and his heart.

photo by Betsy A. Riley

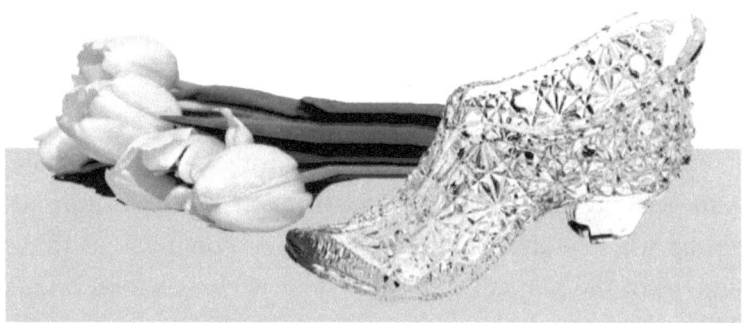

collage by Betsy A. Riley, tulip photo by Larisa Larisa

THE GLASS SLIPPER ARRANGEMENT
by Delfina Hex

The shoe-shaped glass vase was turning out to be good luck for artist Cindy Reddie. She had been cutting some dried thistles to use in a still life, when she spotted the glass slipper. It was partly hidden by the grass at the edge of the paved shoulder. Cindy was amazed that the delicate-looking cut glass had not been cracked or chipped. She had seen miniatures of similar design, but this one was life-sized and deliciously detailed. She tucked the find in the side of her basket and cut a few more thistles, adding some daisies before heading back to her car.

Cindy was an artist, working primarily in watercolors. She had planned to paint an arrangement of thistles and daisies in a milk white ceramic pitcher, but decided to use the glass slipper as a vase instead. The resulting painting was charming. She did several more, positioning the slipper at different angles and rearranging the flowers. The glass slipper watercolors were the first to sell at the weekly art market.

Over the next few months, she did more still life pieces featuring the glass slipper, using violets, sweet pea vines, and wild roses. The old fashioned flowers were even more becoming to the glass slipper than the thistles and daisies. She began scanning her paintings and offering them as prints to keep up with the demand. She got lots of commissions to do paintings of the slipper holding the flowers chosen for a bride's wedding bouquet. She collected the twelve most popular versions into a calendar, and offered it for sale on the internet. From that she got a commission to do an illustration for a magazine targeted to antique shop owners.

A month later she got a late afternoon call from a Mr. Prinz, asking directions to her studio and agreeing on a time to come by the next day. Sylvia Martin showed up just as Cindy was writing down the message and noted the funny look on her friend's face. Sylvia was there to pickup more framed copies of her prize-winning shot from last year's photo safari to Antelope canyon. She'd had the amazing luck to catch a hummingbird in the famous beam of light that pierced the slot canyon at noon. Sylvia was in a great mood, she had just gotten a major catalog commission for the hummingbird photo.

Sylvia had brought a bottle of wine to celebrate, so Cindy got out the glasses. As they were toasting each other's good fortune for the second time, Sylvia asked about the phone message. Cindy shoved the pad Sylvia's way while she refilled her own wine glass. Sylvia took one look at the note and laughed out loud.

"This is priceless," she said between whoops of laughter, "you have an appointment with Mr. Hansen Prinz--get it, it even sounds like Handsome Prince. And he's coming because you have the glass slipper. Face it Cindy Reddie, this is your Cinderella moment." She hiccoughed, "that's means I'll be your Fairy Godmother and help you get dressed for the Ball!"

Cindy waved a dismissal and took another drink of wine. But Sylvia persisted, "Come on Cindy, you have to try on the glass slipper!" The vase was sitting in the middle of her work table, with a dried arrangement in it. Sylvia dumped the flowers on the table and wiped the inside of the vase with a soft cloth. "Come on girl, give me your foot." Cindy laughed, kicked off her Croc and extended her right foot to Sylvia. Surprisingly, her foot slipped right into the vase and fit surprisingly well, as if it had been made for her.

At first she was afraid to put her weight on it, but the leaded crystal was quite sturdy. Maybe that's why it survived a toss onto the roadside without any damage. Cindy held on to the back of a chair and gradually put weight on the foot wearing the glass slipper, Once she had her full weight on it with no problem, she took a few tentative steps. Sylvia applauded and ran to get a camera from her car and snapped several photos.

They finished Sylvia's bottle of wine and started on another. Sylvia had already surrendered her car keys and Cindy had offered her use of the couch upstairs for the night. The ladies ascended the stairs unsteadily and collapsed on the bed and sofa. Cindy tried to pull off the glass slipper, but it seemed stuck. "Hey, Fairy Godmother, a little help here."

Sylvia staggered over and examined the slipper. Funny, the fluted top seemed much higher on Cindy's ankle than when she put it on. Sylvia tugged and tugged, but only succeeded in chafing Cindy's ankle. "I think we need to wait till morning, just prop it up on pillows so your foot doesn't swell."

Morning was no improvement. Both women had headaches and Cindy's foot was beginning to look swollen. Sylvia made coffee while Cindy plunged the slippered foot into a bucket of ice water. It was so cold it hurt, but the shoe was tight as ever, and now her foot was slightly blue. She hoped it was because of the cold, rather than lack of circulation. Sylvia made a pot of coffee, then left to run errands, promising to come back after the Prinz appointment to take Cindy to the doctor.

Cindy freshened up and put on a long skirt to camouflage the slipper. She sorted through her shoes to find one with a heel height that matched the glass slipper so she could at least walk evenly. Downstairs, in her studio, she arranged her latest paintings on tabletop easels, and set out a stack of the calendars.

Mr. Prinz showed up promptly at ten, carrying a copy of the antiques magazine that carried her illustration. Cindy's first thought was how disappointed Sylvia would be. He wasn't the least bit handsome. In fact, he looked rather like her accountant. He asked her to autograph the magazine illustration, which she thought was silly, then asked if she had any more illustrations that were similar. Cindy showed him the new pieces she had set on display, and the many others hanging on the walls of her studio. Judging by the way his eyes darted around, she was sure he was really interested in seeing the vase itself, not just paintings of it.

"It has been nice meeting you, Mr. Prinz," she said, "I always enjoy meeting fans of my work. Was there anything else you wanted?" If she was lucky, he'd buy a print or two and leave. His shifty eyes were giving her the creeps.

"Well, um," he stammered, taken aback by her directness, "I had hoped to see the vase that was your inspiration for these pieces. I collect glassware and might be interested in purchasing it."

"Well I'm not interested in selling it," Cindy said firmly, "It has become sort of a good luck charm for me, and its inspiration for my art has really boosted sales."

"Perhaps you don't realize just how valuable such a piece might be," he said, "especially for a matching pair," He quoted a figure that made her gasp. "That's why I would like to examine the vase, to see if it is indeed one of the particular set I'm seeking."

Cindy laughed, "Sorry to disappoint you, but I only have the one, and it may not be collectible at all after this day is over." She pulled up the hem of her skirt to display the glass slipper, firmly encasing her slightly blue foot. Prinz's hands reached out, as if to snatch it off her foot, but the sound of a slamming car door caused him to draw back.

"Fairy Godmother to the rescue!" Sylvia called out as she entered the studio, laden with shopping bags, "Why you must be Mr. Prinz, so nice to meet you." She swept past him to set the bags on the work table. From behind his back, she flashed a gagging face at Cindy. "You know Timbo? The guy who makes the candlesticks out of old wine bottles? He's loaned me a bunch of glass cutting tools, and I think we can do this in a way that will let you glue it back together, so you can keep on adding to your still life series."

"That's wonderful, Sylvia," Cindy said, anxious to get rid of Mr. Prinz, "Of course it will ruin the collectible value of the glassware, but I am rather fond of my foot." She directed a pointed look at Mr. Prinz, "Now if you will excuse us?" He hesitated, but Sylvia took him by the arm and walked him to the door, chattering nonsense the whole way. She all but pushed him out the entrance, and locked the door behind him.

"What a slug! Handsome Prince indeed!" Sylvia laughed and shook her head, "now let's get a look at that foot of yours." Cindy pulled a couple of chairs to the work table and sat down, propping her foot on a chair. Sylvia pulled up another chair and studied the glass slipper, turning Cindy's foot back and forth carefully. She glanced over at the paintings on the table, then took a harder look. She grabbed one of the calendars and held it next to Cindy's foot.

"What are you doing?" Cindy said, "just get the darned thing off. If you cut the sole at the arch, and then up the sides where the seams would be on a cowboy boot, then it should come apart in two pieces."

"Look!" Sylvia demanded. She hoisted Cindy's foot in the air, almost pulling her off her seat, and brandished the calendar next to the foot. At Cindy's puzzled look, Sylvia flipped the calendar upside down. "Look at the slipper in the painting -- see the fluted rim, how it curls down all around and splits open on the instep?" Cindy nodded, but with that look on her face said she was humoring a crazy person. "Look at the shoe on your foot -- no fluting, no split. The glass changed shape after you put the slipper on!"

As if the implications of that sank in, Sylvia let go of the slipper as if it was burning her fingers. Cindy was barely able to keep her balance as her foot was suddenly released. She sat up slowly and bent her knee to bring the foot in for closer scrutiny. "You're right," she said, looking at the glass wrapped tight above her ankle, "it IS different. No wonder I can't pull my foot back out." She sighed, "At least I don't feel so stupid now, but I really wish it would just open back up. Besides getting my foot out, it was prettier with the fluted edge."

Cindy felt a slight tingle, as the top of the shoe rolled out into the original split fluted edge. Sylvia gasped as Cindy easily slipped her foot free and held the restored vase in her hands. "What just happened?" Cindy said, "I can't believe the thing just opened up."

"You made a wish, that's what happened," Sylvia said. "Quick, put it back on and make another wish."

"Not on your life," Cindy said, turning the glass slipper curiously in her hands, "what if it only gives one wish, and you need that one to get the darned thing back off. I don't want to risk getting my foot stuck in it again."

"Well, maybe it works just holding it in your hands," Sylvia insisted, "wish for something and see."

"Okay," Cindy said, "I wish I had a cinnamon bagel," she paused and looked around expectantly, "See, nothing. What, were you expecting a bagel to drop out of thin air? You're letting this Fairy Godmother stuff go to your head."

"Actually," Sylvia said, "I don't know if that's a fair test." She dragged over one of the shopping bags and pulled out a bakery box of cinnamon bagels. "Of course I know that's your favorite, so I brought them to celebrate after we got the shoe off. Wish for something else."

"Nope, I'm done with that foolishness. Come on, the shoe is off, so let's celebrate now," Cindy set the shoe on the work table and grabbed a bagel to munch on. Sylvia joined her, but there was a faraway look in her eyes. They finished off the bagels and Cindy began to set up another still life to paint.

"You know," Sylvia said, "we should have known Mr. Hansen Prinz was wrong from the start."

"And why is that?" Cindy said, picking up a towel to buff the fingerprints off the glass slipper before filling it with the latest flower arrangement.

"Well, he was searching for both glass slippers," Sylvia said, "the REAL prince is supposed to have one glass slipper and be searching for its mate -- to be HIS mate. Right now, your true love could be holding the matching slipper and searching for you. Ooh, I know--the slipper could have been in his family for generations, and then he sees your painting of its mate in that art journal . . .you know, the one that had the really cute photo of you. He'll track you down -- easy for him because he's filthy rich of course -- and one day he'll show up at your door with the slipper in his hand."

"Yeah, right," Cindy said, snorting, "Like some snooty rich guy is gonna be interested in a simple watercolor artist."

"Okay, YOU decide what your perfect man would be," Sylvia said, "I'm just saying that the slipper is magic and is going to draw him to you. Someday soon there'll be a knock at your door and it will be your true love, and you'll live happily ever after."

"Yeah, I wish," said Cindy, setting the vase on a sapphire blue drape, before filling it with forget-me-nots.

The knock at her door came two weeks later.

photo by Betsy A. Riley

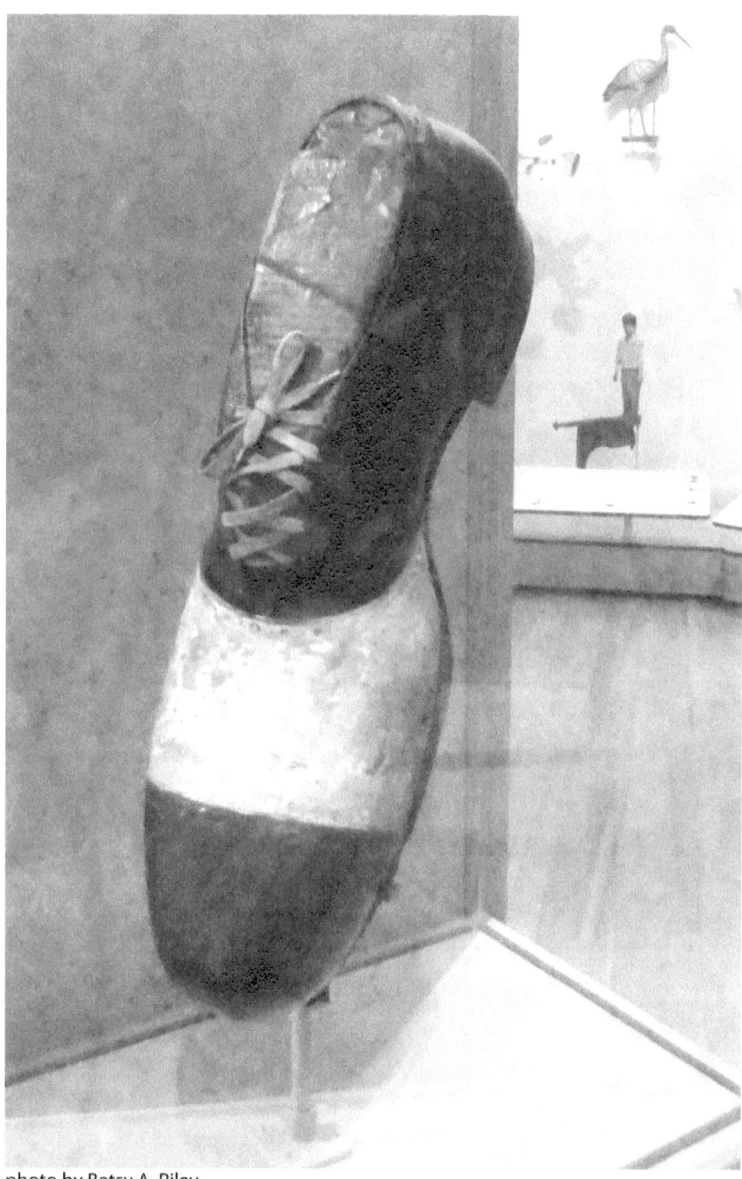

photo by Betsy A. Riley

 **Jack B. Downs** lives in Eldersburg, Maryland, with his wife, Jennifer, and his three sons. His first mystery novel, ***Buried Treasure***, will debut from Apprentice House in late 2012. His short stories have appeared *in Ascent Aspirations* and *Nuvein*. He is a professor of English and Technical Writing, and conducts corporate training classes in writing and project management. He is also active in ecotourist activities in the mid-Atlantic region. Jack moderates a novel and short story critique group in Eldersburg, and is a member of the Maryland Writers Association.

Jack's entry, "*As the Crow Flies*," is post-apocalyptic.

photo by Debra Eloise

AS THE CROW FLIES

by Jack B. Downs

A keening wind pierced the thin branches of the locust tree. The void-black crow hunched, coiling, and then lifted into the air, dark eyes scanning the slate-gray clouds scudding low. Somewhere beyond the billow, a sun rose over the quiet countryside.

The crow arced without effort into the stiff chill. The lane several hundred feet below stretched back into piles of neat, squared stone and glass. Forward, it meandered a distance to a shoreline, and drilled into more piles of the shiny, boxed glass, splintering into smaller and narrower lanes.

In the crow's youth, the lane had been a frenzy of malodorous motion. Shining metal racing faster than the chicken hawk, emitting a defensive scent effective for fending off predators. On occasion, the odd objects would careen headlong into each other, spewing forth undigested life forms, which, instead of fleeing, would stagger about or lie motionless, bleeding out.

Before the life forms could provide sustenance, another metal object ate them, incandescent strobes blinking like the firefly. The wounded and twisted metal elements were hauled away by the worker ants of the species.

As the crow ate and spawned and hunted in the rising and the falling of the sun, the cacophony on the lane slowed, first to a steady stream, then to a trickle. One day, the lane sat dormant, a dry streambed bereft of movement. The surrounding forest, once chattery with the squirrel and the owl and the turkeys and the crickets, also stilled, like a bear settling into hibernation. Prey tottered apparently unwounded, gasping and heaving. Death was everywhere on the land.

The crow at first feasted. But the meat held a strong, fermented tang, not unlike the odor from the contesting metal bugs on the black lane. For a time, the crow huddled, limp and shivering, in the leeward branches of the locust, barely hanging to the tree when the wind kicked and whistled.

The crow expected to plummet, fluttering to the earth far below, as so many of its kind had. But slowly, as it nibbled at whatever skittered up and down the tree trunk, its strength returned. The tiny crawling creatures with the hard shells, shiny violet-black like the crow's own sheen, seemed unaffected by the poison.

The crow, when it had the strength to fly again, rinsed carrion in pools of water. Occasionally, it would lay scraps of meat torn from a carcass onto an ant mound, watching as the army of tiny clickers consumed the outer edges of the scrap. Then the crow would rush forward, wings unsheathed, scatter the ants, and retrieve the remainder.

One day, after the passing of several wide-and-narrow moons, the crow spied a two-legged creature emerging from within the boxes by the shore. It staggered as if ill, one moment poised to turn off the lane, pausing on wavering legs. The next moment it lurched toward the forest, roughly within the borders of the lane.

The few remaining residents of the wood paused, in their collecting and their chattering, to consider the passage of this apex creature. In the crow's small and active brain, some dim sparking conjured a memory of the beings occasionally ejected from the long-ago metal bugs. The crow felt no fear. No urge to flee downrange. This creature aroused no feel of danger. To the contrary, the crow sensed this staggering wraith would soon be sustenance.

The two-legged creature shuffled, beak down, without a hint of alertness about it. The crow had witnessed creatures capable of feigning illness, or even death, to avert predators. However, this animal seemed to be dead without realizing it. The crow had seen that too.

The apex creature stumbled to all fours on oddly hinged legs. The leg joint bent forward, not back. The result of some vicious attack? The crow gazed, mildly curious, as the animal with the strange coat slowly rose again, leaving behind an oddly shaped clump of leather and sinew. The crow noted that the creature's other leg was bound in a similar mass. It must not be an imperative body part, for the space between the creature and the strange mass grew in the creature's slow progress down the lane.

The crow watched, eyes hooded, as the lame mammal faltered on the blacktop lane. Suddenly with more vigor than the crow would have thought possible, the creature's body flexed rigid. The mammal arched, face skyward, as if struck by a jagged bolt of fire from the clouds. The creature raised its forelegs high above its head, eyes wide, and cried out in a strange cry. The call was unlike any the crow had heard before, perhaps a bit like a bear's, but more keening. A cry of pain, rather than of bluster, with rapid lip movements and a biting rasp, as if it interrupted itself.

With a final shiver that convulsed it from the tips of its fingers to its odd back legs, the creature suddenly relaxed and dropped forward onto its face.

For a moment, all was still, as if the forest itself had gasped its last. Then the crow noted movement under the low bushes at the edge of the lane. Darting, then retreat. Sniffing and tentative pawing. The smaller woodland mammals approached the lifeless husk, tentative, skittish, then emboldened. Prey became predators. The spent apex creature eventually vanished in a flurry of feasting. The celebration lasted for several sunrises and sunsets. The crow was content to nibble at the periphery, and then return to its aerie post, a lone sentry to the passing.

Finally, it was as if the sickly mammal had never passed below. Flesh and sinew had first been rent, then ripped, then nibbled, and finally atomized. Bones were snuffled, and furtively spirited away, to be gnawed under the low growth. After a season, the fabric was picked apart, the brighter colors adorning the nests of robins and blue jays, and even the crow's.

The crow swooped from the south and touched lightly on the deserted and cracking blacktop, tenacious thistles and stalks poking up through numerous cracked and crumbled spots. The bird bounced inquisitively around the one remaining artifact of the last apex animal. The covering had slipped from the nearer foot of the mammal as it headed away from the sea, to the setting sun. Now it lay at the side of the lane, half covered by leaves and sprouting moss.

The crow picked at it, sampling the fare. The skin was leathery, a cow's flayed skin. Quickly disinterested, the crow lifted itself with a powerful flap, and circled south to its perch.

Collage by Betsy A. Riley from photos by Debra Eloise